Blood & Sex

Michael

Angela Cameron

ra**V**enous
romance™

RED SILK
EDITIONS

First published in paperback in 2010 by
Red Silk Editions
an imprint of Red Wheel/Weiser, LLC
with offices at:
500 Third Street, Suite 230
San Francisco, CA 94107

First published as an e-book in 2009 by
Ravenous Romance
100 Cummings Center
Suite 123A
Beverly, MA 01915
www.ravenousromance.com

ISBN: 978-1-59003-203-9
Library of Congress Cataloging-in-Publication Data available upon request.

Cover design by April Martinez
Cover photograph © Literary Partners Group, Inc.

Printed in Canada
TCP
10 9 8 7 6 5 4 3 2 1

The paper used in this publication meets the minimum requirements of the American National Standard for Information Sciences—Permanence of Paper for Printed Library Materials Z39.48-1992 (R1997).

Chapter One

VICTORIA TYLER knelt in front of the nude corpse in the dark alley between the worn brick buildings of Third Street, the home of Collins Bay's strip clubs, peep shows, and tattoo parlors. She managed to tune out the traffic roaring down the streets that met the alley on either side, but when the scent of blood and garbage wafted upward on the sudden breeze, her stomach flipped. She breathed out hard, just like she always did to clear the smell of death from her nose, and fought back the twinge of nausea.

Her hand was steady as she used the slim metal pointer to move a blood-matted clump of long blonde hair away from the corpse's neck. She saw a big bruise that matched the others that were scattered across the body. She aimed the flashlight at the spot, but couldn't tell exactly how old the injury was. The mix of hot days and cool nights could do strange things to a body in Florida in October.

Another dark spot peeked out from beneath the girl's arm, and Tori gently raised it for a better look. Just to the left of the breast was a circle of bloody dots and dashes, with long trails of fluid that crusted on the skin. She'd bet they'd find more bruises, just like this one, when the body wasn't slumped beside a dumpster on a cloud-covered night. After all, the bite marks were why the newspaper had given the killer the name "Bay Gnasher."

Footsteps shuffled behind her. She glanced up and saw Joe Phillips looking over her shoulder. Joe was one of Collins' finest, a clean cut uniform with dark hair that remained in a perpetual crew cut. He was a little cheesy and a few brain cells short of detective material, but he seemed nice enough. He'd been with the force for years, even before she started, and tried to downplay his interest in crime scene investigation, but they all knew. It was hard not to know when he never stopped talking about those damned forensics shows on television.

Tori shook her head to fight back a smile that tickled her lips, and then motioned to the mark. "What does this look like to you, Joe?"

He hovered over her shoulder, and his uniform pressed against her back. If he'd been anyone else, she'd have clocked him for invading her space. "Bite marks?"

"Looks like it." She glanced again at the woman's wrist, where a hunk of flesh was missing, then to what was left of a youthful face. *Such a shame.* "You said no one was around when you found her, right?"

"Yeah."

Tori stood so quickly that Joe stumbled back to dodge her shoulder.

"Alright, get statements from everyone who is within sight of this dumpster, including those apartments." She pointed down the alley, toward another brick building that erupted from the concrete at the opposite end. "If they're not home, come back tomorrow. Right now, we have nothing and this guy's got eight victims in two months. I don't think he plans to slow down anytime soon."

"We'll get on it, Tori."

She gave him a pat on the shoulder. If they did great work, they'd save her a lot of time. "I know you will"

She didn't watch Joe turn, but heard his clinking footsteps move toward a cluster of cops drinking coffee and laughing about something, probably a dirty joke. She glanced around once more and saw something glinting from under the edge of the dumpster. She bent and pulled it forward with her pointer.

It was a key with a smooth black plastic tag and shiny silver ring. She fished the metallic point through the ring and balanced it closer to her face. Stamped on the tag, in blood red, was a three-part symbol similar to a yin-yang. A private room key from *The Scene*. She shook her head and sighed. Of all the places to be involved, a club for vampire BDSM junkies hadn't been on her short list, especially one with a reputation for being the last location of so many missing persons.

"What's that? Find something?"

Tori folded the key ring into her hand and closed the pointer for distraction. She turned her head and saw Joe squinting from the edge of a crowd of officers.

"Nothing. Just a piece of garbage." She tucked both into her jacket pocket and moved toward the group.

Vampiro involvement was one thing, but *The Scene* was out of her league. She'd have to call in some help. She shivered at the thought. Those walking leeches couldn't be trusted, not one of them, but going into that club without a *dominatore* was just plain asking for it. She was the only unbound human in the city with knowledge of them. She didn't plan to become one of their mindless goons anytime soon.

* * * *

Michael snaked through the crowd, watching Damon, the protégé of the city's head vampire, towering over the figure of a frail young girl in some Goth getup against the far wall.

He could smell her fear, even across the room. It mixed with the scent of warming female flesh and made his teeth ache.

He shook his head, trying to swallow down his hunger. In spite of the thumping music, he could hear her pulse hammering under her thin veil of skin. The monster inside him trained on the sound, and his mouth watered.

Her thoughts came to him in swift flashes. She'd lied, used the fake ID, and now she wished she hadn't. The pale guy with dark eyes and hair wouldn't leave her alone. She couldn't make herself walk away, or even turn her eyes away from him.

Michael forced the thoughts away, and then watched Damon lean down toward the girl's neck. His hand spread wide on her shoulder. The fool wouldn't bite her in the club, would he? He couldn't. He knew the rules.

He walked faster. If the humans weren't so close, he could stop Damon in an instant. But they were, and their safety mattered above all else. Plus, the *Alleanza* called for the death of any who revealed their true nature to humans. The girl was important, but stopping Damon from feeding in public wasn't exactly worth being hunted and drained.

The warm metallic scent of blood sprayed through the air. Pale faces in the crowd turned toward the couple. Michael's own blood pounded in his ears, his face began to burn, and his teeth lengthened. He breathed in, forced the hunger back, fired up the anger within him, and then threw it at the man's back like a dagger. He saw Damon stumble forward, and rushed toward them as fast as he could without spooking the humans.

Damon glared over his shoulder. "Back off."

Michael's voice came out as a growl, but he managed to keep it low. "Leave the girl and go back to Castillo. You've broken the *Alleanza* more than once tonight."

He released the girl so fast that she stumbled against the wall. Locks of red and black hair quickly fell in front of the two neat holes in her neck, hiding them from the humans.

When he turned to face Michael, they were almost eye-to-eye, although Damon's bodybuilder physique made him appear much larger. "Are you threatening me, boy?"

There was a push of his dark power, and Michael answered it with a bigger push. "I'll make it a fucking promise if you don't get out of my face."

"Castillo would have your head."

"You won't live long enough to tell him."

The man blinked and Michael felt a quick flash of his fear.

"You can be replaced, Michael. He relies on my word, and my word says that you're nothing more than a hired gun."

"But he depends on my power."

Damon smiled, but it didn't reach his eyes. "Let me have this one and all is forgiven."

Michael leaned forward, bumping the man's chest. "Leave now and I'll pretend that you didn't just try to bribe the *Garante*."

The man's eyes searched his. Michael could feel the press of power that searched for a crack in his resolve. He wouldn't find one. It had been years since he'd had a sense of self-preservation. Now, no one threatened him without backing it up. So far, no one had actually managed to live up to their threat, except for Castillo.

"Boys." Christine, that brown haired angel in a red dress, crooned and hooked her slender arms through theirs. "The night is young. Don't deny the ladies the feel of your teeth on their throats tonight."

Damon's shoulders relaxed only a little. Michael gave him one last glare. "Take him, but make sure he stays away from the humans."

She nodded and kissed Michael on the cheek. "As you wish, my *padrone.*"

He watched her escort the idiot toward the private rooms, while he slid the dizzy human into a seat. He'd kill that *leggero* one day. One day when Castillo wasn't the ruler of this city.

* * * *

Tori gripped the steering wheel of her Jeep and fought the urge to throw the phone out the window onto the damp pavement. Instead, she listened to the sound of Chief Ives' breath coming in long draws and watched as her headlights illuminated one street sign after another.

"Have you seen the papers today? They're calling for my resignation. You know that if this doesn't work, you're off the lead. We're up to eight bodies, Tyler, and I'm getting pretty fucking tired of having my ass bit off for you."

"I know, Chief. I'll handle it. I'm close. I'm going to meet with another contact this evening." She steered into the parking lot between an abandoned warehouse and Michael's club, which looked like any other old warehouse from the outside, except for the red neon sign on the building that simply said *The Fallen.*

"Make this work. You've got one week."

"I will. Gotta go." She clicked the phone shut and tossed it into the passenger's seat.

Her heart thumped in her throat until it became a knot that threatened to choke her. Nobody needed to remind her what was at stake. That's why she'd come to this hellhole of a club in the first place. Sam, her vampire informant, made it very clear that Michael was the only one who would and could help her. *Damn him.*

She stepped out, slammed the door, and clicked the remote over her shoulder, locking the doors with a honk that reverberated off the block walls around her. She straightened her black skirt and black halter-top, and hoped she didn't look like a prostitute. That was another reason not to be here. She didn't dress in a skirt for anyone she didn't want to sleep with. Still, here she was, headed to see that jerk, and in a damned skirt no less. *God, there'd better be a promotion in all this.*

She went for the sidewalk, hung a left at the corner of the building, and then weaved through the crowd that waited to enter near the door. Strange bodies brushed hers. Perfumes mingled with the smell of sweat and marijuana in the air, creating a sickening sweet smell that made her wrinkle her nose.

"Hey, don't shove, bitch."

She jerked her head around to see an awkward, pimpled boy decorated in black, wiry tattoos and silver piercings. He looked like a nerd trying to reverse his position as the football team's whipping boy by going Goth. *Figures.*

His eyes widened, but he threw out his chest and stood a little straighter, as if the height made a difference.

She moved toward him. "What did you say to me?"

The kid's mouth gaped open.

His friend elbowed him. "Dude, she's hot."

She shot the shorter guy a warning look and moved closer. "Did you call me a bitch?"

"Uh. Yeah." He lifted his chin so that it topped her head. "Yeah, I did."

He was too tall for a clear punch, so she drew back a foot and landed the blunt tip of her shoe in his nuts. "Fuck you."

His short friend howled in laughter as the lanky kid crumpled onto the concrete.

Tori turned and moved toward the door again. She pushed a few more people out of the way and finally stood in front of two burly men in black shades and T-shirts that had logos matching the sign and *SECURITY* written on the sleeves. The shades, though—she'd never quite figured out why nocturnal monsters would wear sunglasses. *Go figure.*

Gregory was the one with bleached blond spikes and a silver hoop in his ear. Blaine's dark hair had fluorescent green tips that glistened in the moonlight. Together, they looked more like bodybuilders than real fighters, but they made a nice wall of muscle.

"Detective Tyler." Gregory smiled, and she caught a flash of white fang. "What brings you here?"

"I need to talk with Michael."

Blaine laughed. "Man, I knew you'd be back. You can't li—"

Tori threw up a hand. "Don't start. I'm here on official business."

He pulled his shades down his nose with one finger and looked at her over the top. "Well, if that's the new uniform, daddy likey?"

She shook her head and groaned. "Just let me in, Blaine."

Gregory shook his head. "I don't know. I think we'd better check with the boss. Last time you caused a shitstorm."

"If you don't let me in, I'll bring the whole force down here to investigate the two underage kids I just saw go in." She hadn't really seen any go in, but Blaine had a habit of letting in the girls he planned to hit on later. They were usually blond, clean, and right out of Catholic school.

They glanced at each other.

Gregory said, "Alright. We'll let him know you're here."

"Try not to kill anyone tonight." Blaine shook his head and pulled one of the heavy steel doors open. Metal music poured onto the sidewalk.

Tori nodded and stepped inside. The door slammed behind her. She stood still, waiting for her eyes to adjust to the darkness. Michael probably already knew she was here. With all that telepathy floating around, who could tell what they did and didn't know?

"Miss Tyler."

She turned to see a statuesque woman in a black latex French maid costume smiling down at her from behind the coat check window. "Your gun."

Shit. She'd really hoped to sneak in with it, but they always knew. Did they see it? Of course not. Maybe it was that she always had a gun. She slipped the gun out of the back of her skirt and handed it to the girl, grip first. "Just don't scratch it up, Susan."

"Thank you." The girl winked her dark shadowed eye and slid the gun under the counter. "I'll keep it warm and cozy just for you."

Something in the way that she said it made Tori shiver. When another leather-laden couple approached, she slipped away toward the double doors. A tiny girl in red leather pushed through ahead of her and sent a rush of heavy rhythms through the room. With the deafening sound came the sweet smells of sex, alcohol, and smoke of various kinds. Bleach faintly lingered with it, followed by something metallic. Blood?

Tori stepped through to the edge of a small ocean of bodies that writhed in time under flashing lights, like a leather orgy. She weaved toward a table in the darkest back corner. She needed the darkness, especially in here. The less people saw of her, when half of the city wanted her head on a stake, the better.

When she slid onto the smooth leather stool at the high table, she felt eyes on her, the eyes of people that probably could read her mind—and probably were. Shit. This was a bad idea. She should've come after hours when the humans were gone and there was no pretending, but even that was risky. Why did the *vampiro* always make her feel more like the vegetable of the day on the menu at Bruno's Diner than a cop?

"Ya want a drink, honey?" Jude, a gum-smacking waitress with short magenta hair, came forward and leaned her arms on the table as she bent toward Tori's face. Her breasts were full and threatened to spill out over the rim of the black corset she was wearing.

Even to a straight girl like Tori, it was distracting. She pulled her hand away from the girl's to give it a little distance. "Hey, Jude. Margarita—and tell Jack I said no funny business, okay? Just a plain margarita."

"Well, you're no fun tonight."

"I had a little too much fun last time."

A wicked grin spread across the girl's dark lips. "You did, didn't you?"

"Yeah, let's just keep it simple tonight."

"Suit yourself." The girl shrugged and walked away.

Tori wiped a pearl of sweat off her brow and leaned back against the chair. She was warm, but her core felt cool, almost chilled. Something about this place always made her feel hot and cold at the same time. Maybe it was another vampire *trucchi*.

* * * *

The lights dimmed and the music faded. People moved to their seats in the darkness, as an intoxicating voice boomed through the room. It slid over Tori's skin like silk and made her heart flutter. More vampire tricks.

Nothing good ever came from asking vampires for help. It was always the same thing. Michael tried to get in her pants, she got pissed, and someone got hurt. Tori leaned back in the chair and crossed her legs.

"Please welcome to the stage," the voice said, rising almost to a yell, "Vlad."

She stifled a laugh and shook her head. That was rich. Jonas, Michael's right-hand man, had been the opening act on Fridays for as long as she'd known about the place, but she'd never noticed that his stage name was homage to the original vampire.

"What's so funny?" Jude sat a tall green glass with a thick salt rim on the table.

Tori took the drink, sniffing it suspiciously. "Nothing."

Jude glanced toward the stage and rested an elbow on the table. "God, he's easy on the eyes."

Tori took a sip of the margarita. First was the taste of the lime and tequila, warming her throat as it went down. When she sat the glass down and licked her lips, the salt from the rim made her mouth water.

"Have you seen the new act?" Jude didn't look back.

"No."

She laughed. "Oh. You're in for a treat. He'll try to roll you, ya know?" Jack whistled from the bar, and Jude nodded in his direction. "Gotta run. If you need anything, gimme a yell."

"Thanks." She took another sip as the woman walked away.

The music flared to a pounding rock rhythm. A strobe light began its eye-aching flash from behind the stage curtain, silhouetting a tall male figure with a woman curled around his leg. One second there was nothing, the next they were just standing there. It wasn't so much magic as an optical illusion, or at least that's what they wanted people to think.

The curtains parted and Jonas yanked the woman to stand with her back to him. He was as handsome as ever. His sandy hair was almost to his shoulders now and he wore it pushed away from his face. The muscles in his upper arms bulged out from the black wife-beater shirt with gray watercolor words on it. He had on the handful of bracelets that he always wore, which would have made most men look foolish, but added to his overall ferocity somehow. Adding to the cliché rocker image that he loved were the tribal-looking tattoos that decorated his neck and crawled up the side of his face and down his arm.

The vampire magnified the woman's emotions and amplified them toward the audience, who sat on edge. A band suddenly appeared behind them, matching music to the movements. Slowly, the woman moved behind him and her hands ran up his waist. As he began to belt out the words to the song in a sexy, sleepy voice, the woman ran her hands up and down his zipper. Lust crashed through the room, and when he moaned, the audience shifted and moaned with him, captive to the vampiric influence.

One hand caught in the woman's hair, Jonas yanked her head to the side, arching that vein toward him. In between lyrics, she kissed his arm, hungry for him. He took the need, balled it up and threw it at the audience like a psychic bomb.

Tori felt it too, like a lover's hand between her legs. She dug her nails further into her skin. She wouldn't feel this, not this cheap thrill. It was another way that they took control, turning their prey into bite junkies who lived for the next donation.

Jonas stared at her for a long moment, then flashed a quick wink.

Shit. He knew she wasn't letting go. He pulled the woman's arm to his mouth. His words mixed with actions so that it looked planned, but Tori knew it wasn't. Michael would never allow a public feeding on stage.

He stepped in front of the girl and teased his way up her arm so that the group could watch and feel every tingling tease. Evil bastard.

A woman in the audience cried, "Yes!"

When his teeth scraped over the girl's skin, he rolled his eyes toward Tori—and she didn't look away.

Even pain couldn't stop the feel of Jonas' teeth on her skin. Everything inside her screamed to go to him. His voice called to her inside her mind, and her body ached for the reality his show promised.

She gasped and leaned forward, gripping the table. He smiled as if he'd felt her break, and then closed his mouth over the woman's wrist. The ghostly sharp points of his fangs pressed against the skin of Tori's neck.

Chapter Two

"VICTORIA?" THE voice was a pure indulgence that promised to rob a woman of her senses.

Tori glanced up in that direction and saw Michael staring across the table at her. He reminded her of an Italian model with messy dark hair. The crystalline blue eyes added to the effect, contrasting sharply with his dark shadow of facial hair, even though he was clean-shaven. His body was still that of a strong warrior, even though he hadn't ridden into battle in centuries.

He leaned closer. The smell of him drifted toward her. "Tori, are you alright? You look a bit shaken."

It was a spicy sandalwood scent with a hint of something she couldn't quite pinpoint. Vanilla maybe? Either way, it was fascinating, and made her want to lean closer, to inhale at the collar of his starched white shirt. Instead, she nodded and held her hand out to shake his. "I'm fine, Michael. How—how are you?"

He glanced down, smiled, and then took the offered hand in his. He flipped it over to reveal the bloody palm and raised it to his mouth. She wanted to pull back, but it would've been the ultimate insult; one that could get her killed. She'd offered a blood greeting, even if it was by accident, and now she was committed.

* * * *

Michael's tongue slid slowly across Tori's palm and took the bit of blood she offered with a slow and easy pace. She tasted like the warm blackberry wine his father used to drink, and it tingled as it slid down his throat. The scent of her excitement rose to blend with the blood and he considered taking a second lick. If he did, she'd probably try to kill him again.

"A surprising greeting from you." Michael slipped into the chair beside her. "I assume that there's something you want from me."

As soon as his lips left her skin, she pulled the small hand back and tucked it under the table. She was as attractive as ever, though a little thinner than he'd like. Before, when they first met, she had the shapely, round hips and fuller breasts that he stared at for so long from the shadows. Now, she was leaner, but still as enticing. Her dark hair had grown longer, even though she kept it pulled back in that ridiculous ponytail. It was just enough to make him want to reach across and pop that band out so that it fell free.

"Right, as usual." She straightened her back and stared at him with those pale green eyes that contrasted so starkly with her black lashes.

"Is it safe to assume that it has something to do with your serial killer?"

"If you can read my mind, why don't you just cut the crap and answer my question?"

Her eyes wandered back to the stage and he could hear her pulse speeding. Jonas was having an effect on her. Good, she was out of practice.

"I thought that I'd let you keep control, the way you like to do." He folded his arms across his chest and leaned to block the act from her view. When those exotic eyes cut to him, he asked, "What can I do to help our trusty police department?"

She arched a brow at him, and then let it relax. "I need you to get me into *The Scene*."

He laughed. "And why would you need to get in there, my lovely detective?"

"All of my evidence points to a man who works inside the club. If I try to go in undercover, they'll smell me a mile away. I won't even make it to the bar."

"Actually, they'll probably welcome you as a snack, but when they realize you're a cop, they'll take you as one of their *blood mystresses*. Besides, some of Castillo's group will recognize you as Robert's fiancé."

She rolled her eyes. "Thanks for making me feel so much safer."

"Maybe you should do what you normally do. Rush in with your S.W.A.T. team and guns blazing?"

"Because I don't want John Q. Public to know that you guys exist any more than you do. Second, I don't want to get cops killed."

"Slaughtered is more like it."

She nodded.

"I don't think it's a good idea. I'll ask around, perhaps pay Castillo a visit, but stay out of that club until I give you the okay."

"That's not an option, Michael."

He leaned forward. "You don't have a choice."

"You need anything else, hon?" Jude moved up to the table and stood a little too close. Michael leaned back to give her room.

"No, thanks." Tori didn't look at the girl.

"You be careful with Casanova here." She nudged him and gave him a wink. "He can have your clothes off before you even realize he moved."

"I'll keep that in mind." She arched her brow at him.

He didn't allow the grin to spread across his lips. She was edging toward jealousy, but she would never acknowledge it. Still, if she was jealous, and he helped her, she might be a liability. Most of the *cosca* didn't trust her and she was quick to draw that pistol she loved so much.

Michael motioned toward the bar. "Jude, be a dear and let us talk privately."

"Sure thing, boss." The girl slipped away quickly.

Tori nibbled on the edge of her pinkie nail. "Look, I wouldn't be here if I weren't desperate. You know how I feel about all this and I wouldn't step foot back in this hellhole if you weren't my last resort. I'm about to lose my career over this and I have to be the one to find the evidence. You're not a cop."

He leaned back and looked at her. She actually meant every word of that. "If I were a lesser man, I might be offended by that statement."

She pulled the finger away from her mouth, examined it, and then tucked it down to her lap. "Good thing you're not then, huh?"

He nodded and reached toward her neck. Slowly, his hand touched the mound of scar tissue that covered most of her neck beneath her ear, giving her a silent reminder of what she risked. "You are certain that you must be the one to enter the club?"

She pulled away and anger flashed across her face. "Would I be here if I weren't?"

"True." Michael draped his arm over the chair beside him and let his legs fall casually open. "This poses an interesting position for you, Tori. For once, you truly *do* need me."

"Don't get cocky."

"I would never attempt to get cocky with you, *inamorato*."

* * * *

Tori didn't know what that word meant, but it couldn't be good because the way he dragged it out in the Italian accent that made it sound dirty, and he smiled that way, the way he did after he kissed her at the New Year's Eve party. She looked down at her hands quickly and pretended to examine her fingernails. Her face felt warm and she knew she was blushing, but her heart felt like it dropped to her stomach. "Don't do that."

"What?"

"Fuck with my head like that. You know I hate it when you guys do that to me."

"I didn't do anything."

"Liar."

He laughed. "If you feel some attraction to me, it is no manipulation of mine."

"I'm not attracted to you."

He cleared his throat. "You do remember that I can hear when your heartbeat speeds and smell—"

"Alright!" She threw up a hand. "Enough. I get the point."

He laughed again, a full throaty sound that echoed over the music. "Why are you so afraid?"

She threw him a pointed glance, then took a long sip from the margarita and licked the salt from her lips again. Why should she explain it to him again? Wasn't twice enough? Some people just never got it. "So, are you going to help me or not?"

"Do you know who it is?"

Tori couldn't say it aloud, the others would hear. Even a whisper was too loud around super hearing, so she held out her hand and let out a long breath. "Here."

When his hand took hers, it was warm and moist, like a human's. He fed tonight. His power rolled over her like a warm breeze that flowed through her flesh. It brought with it the scent of him, that wonderful spicy scent that made her stomach tighten and her breath catch.

She glanced down at the intertwined hands and tried to remember the name that Sam told her. Was it Damon? *Yeah, Damon.* Sam's face appeared in her mind and she tried to focus on the words he was saying, but instead she started to see the shape of Michael's shoulders. No, it was Michael's shoulders in solid form, and she reached out to him. Her hand slid inside the pressed shirt through the open top button and pressed against his chest.

The image began to fade and she felt Michael's real hand squeeze hers lightly, and then released it, dragging across her skin and pulling a long breath away as they went. *Shit.*

She blinked her eyes open to see him leaning back in his chair with a brow arched at her, the only marker of emotion on an otherwise blank face. He wouldn't have allowed an emotion to seep through, including the brow, if he didn't want her to notice. Vampires could be cold bastards when they wanted to.

"Is it that bad?"

He smiled. "How will the police end their investigation with no killer?"

"Let me handle that."

The smile disappeared suddenly. "Humor me, detective. I am the *Garante* for the *padrone* of this city, after all."

"I have evidence that I can plant on this guy I know that's making snuff films. We've been trying to nail him for a while. This way, the department's got both cases wrapped up in a neat little red bow. If you help, we can even have the creep believing he did it."

He rubbed his chin. "Castillo will protect him."

"I know."

"It won't be easy."

"I don't have a choice, Michael, or I wouldn't be here."

He smiled again, slowly this time. "No, you wouldn't, would you?"

She shrugged her agreement.

"Alright then." He leaned forward and propped his hands on the table. "I will, on one condition."

"Should I ask?"

"I get one taste and with the *affascina*—"

"Hell no!" She threw her hands up, accidentally bumping the glass, but he caught it and set it upright with only a small slosh. "I'm not going to be in your power without a fight."

He licked the drink off his thumb, looked at it strangely, and then smiled at her. "So, there is no deal."

"Come on. Michael, you know why." She smirked. "Besides, I could bust you for so many things that you'd never get out of jail, like selling liquor to minors, the prostitutes that you allow in here…oh, and the drugs that Jonas has been buying off that guy that deals out of here."

"Threaten all you want. If you were going to do it, you already would have. I will only offer this once. My part of the bargain is just to ensure that you finally understand that your *boy* was nothing like me."

She eyed him carefully, watching the triumphant little grin spread across his face. He thought he'd won. There had to be a way out of this.

"You're not going to do it without me. He's too powerful, and I won't allow others to get involved with the life of my *padrone*, the one I'm sworn to protect, on the line."

She stared at him. If there was one vampire that everyone seemed to think remotely resembled an honest person, it was Michael. Of course, all of the *vampiro* played the power games and did what best suited their interests. Plus, he was the most powerful in the area. He was right; she couldn't do it without him.

She sighed and nodded. "Only if you swear you won't molest me or some shit."

He chuckled. "Every time we meet, you act as though I can't resist you. I assure you that I have plenty of female companions."

"That's not a promise."

He laughed harder, and with a nod, added, "I swear to you, I won't do anything while you are enthralled that you don't ask for."

Tori grumbled, "Still not good enough." She pointed at him. "You could suggest it, or have me begging through bl— your influences."

His smile faded. "You're beginning to annoy me."

"You'll get over it."

He placed a hand over his heart, as if that gave the words more validity. "I promise that I will not do anything that you truly do not wish me to do, and I will not bite you. Even when you beg."

She refused to play his game. "Alright. I'll be by tomorrow to get started."

With one last gulp that drained the margarita, she slid from the chair.

"I expect my payment tonight."

"What?"

"You have your promise, which puts me immediately in danger. So I expect payment tonight."

"You're out of your mind."

"Then you have no deal." Michael stood and walked toward the door that she knew led to the V.I.P. section of the club that was reserved for vampires.

Shit. If she let him bite her and mess with her head, she probably wouldn't think straight for days. But she needed him. It wasn't an option. "Michael." She caught up to him as he moved into the other room. "I'll give you half. Just a nibble. No mind games."

He turned to her and a slow grin crept across his face. "I thought you might." He motioned toward a dark booth in the corner. "It will only take a moment."

Tori's heart beat a little faster and her palms grew moist as she reached the table.

"Don't be afraid."

"I'm not."

"Liar." Michael slid into the booth and motioned to the seat beside him.

She slipped in, but kept a little space between them. "How do I know you're going to stop?"

"You don't."

"I want a witness."

He gave her a slight nod, then slipped one arm up on the back of her seat. "Jonas will be here in just a moment."

Dammit. Just what she needed: a witness who wanted her blood as much as he did.

Before she could argue, Jonas entered the room. He was even more gorgeous than he had been on stage. The man was pure sex on legs and he stalked toward her with a devious grin. "So, you're ready to admit how much you want me?"

Tori rolled her eyes. "Let's just get this over with."

Jonas slid in beside her. "What am I going to witness?"

Michael spoke before she did. "She agreed to let me feed once, but she doesn't trust me to stop."

He laughed. "Smart woman."

Michael let out a soft growl.

Jonas shrugged.

"Alright." Tori angled herself toward Michael and arched her neck. "Go ahead."

"I was going for the arm, but if you insist." He slid a warm hand behind her neck and pulled her closer.

When Tori closed her eyes, she inhaled him in one long breath that made her mind feel light and dizzy. He smelled wonderful. The scent of him took her back to that light place where her body wanted him naked against her. Somewhere inside her alarms were going off, but she didn't care. The only thing she cared about was the fact that his other hand was wrapped around her waist, but she wanted it between her legs, massaging the growing throb that made her skin moisten. Her heart thumped and the image of him going down on her filled her mind.

She opened her eyes to expel the vision. "I think I don't—"

The pinprick of fangs hit her skin.

Then his teeth pushed in with a pop that made her gasp. Her mind focused on the mouth and the feel of Michael's waist in her hands. She gripped him, feeling the pull of his mouth on her neck, along with the heat from her blood as it moved into him. Time seemed irrelevant as she melted into his grasp.

Jonas made a gasping noise that reminded her that he was watching. She felt him scoot closer and could feel his eyes on them. His hand went to her wrist. She knew he was checking her pulse, but it gave her the feeling that he wanted to join them.

She heard Jonas say something, but she couldn't make out the words.

Her body jolted. Inside, something broke free and radiated through her in a few quick, intense waves that brought an orgasm that pulled her power and made her feel weak. She heard herself moan from a distance that surprised her and then heard Jonas again.

"Michael," he said in a loud, desperate whisper. "You're going to drain her. Let go."

Another moan left her, but it stopped when something covered her mouth. Slowly, she slid back to her shaking body. Michael's lips were sliding over hers, warm and wet. The kiss was slow and deliberate, sending aftershocks through her body with each flick of his tongue.

His tongue. She was kissing Michael. The vampire.

Tori pulled away quickly and fell against the back of the seat.

Michael blinked at her and Jonas laughed. "You two had some serious mojo workin' there."

"Are you alright?" Michael reached for Tori's shoulder, but she leaned away.

"A nibble! I said a nibble!" Her hand went to her neck quickly.

"I don't—I didn't intend to."

She shook her head. "I think you can consider yourself paid."

Michael nodded and seemed, for the first time, a bit embarrassed.

Jonas touched her shoulder and warmth radiated from the spot. Her body slowly relaxed, and her heart slowed. "I think it's time for me to go home."

Michael nodded, still looking a bit shocked. "Wear something a bit more suitable tomorrow. They will all know who you are and don't trust you. It needs to look like I have some control over you or things could get ugly."

"Alright." Jonas slid from the booth and she started out behind him. She pulled away slowly and took Jonas' offered hand to help her stand. The room tilted a little and then snapped into place. She hoped no one would mistake her for a drunk driver on the ride home.

Michael appeared in front of her and grabbed her wrist. His power rushed up her arm, with words that echoed through her mind. *You do realize that we have to give the appearance of a real couple. Castillo and the others will expect me to be the dominant in any relationship, especially one with a human. You're going to be uncomfortable at times.*

"I know."

"Michael," said a high-pitched female voice.

Tori turned to see a tall blonde whose silicone mounds threatened to fall over the top of her black latex corset. The woman giggled her way over to him with an identical woman in red latex.

He didn't turn, so she said it again. "Michael, come dance with us."

"Pleeeease," the other woman said.

He released Tori's hand, stood, and offered a small bow that reminded her how old he really was. "If you'll excuse me."

"By all means, don't let me hold you back from the bimbo patrol."

He shot her a reprimanding look, then turned toward the women.

She watched as he disappeared into the crowd of dancing figures with one woman on each arm. What was she doing here? She had quite successfully avoided men like him her whole life. Men who believed that women were supposed to fall down and worship them because they were so damned sexy. Arrogant bastard.

* * * *

Michael lay in his bed. He pushed his hands behind his head and stared up at the stone ceiling. The darkness of the room pressed in around him. The coming daybreak felt like a weight on his chest. Before long, if all went according to plan, he would have enough power to stay awake during the daylight hours, too.

He yawned and wiped his eyes. If it worked, they'd be free—his entire *cosca* free to live without being captive to Castillo's psychotic wraths.

Actually, more than that would happen. He'd been pissing everyone off lately. The city leaders were all corrupt and dispensed their own brand of law when the mood suited them, but Castillo was dangerous. Letting Damon run free with his *cosca* was one thing, but to allow him to murder humans—well, that was something different. It might even justify Castillo's death.

If it went perfectly, Michael might even have that enticing little human in his bed to celebrate their newfound freedom. He closed his eyes and felt his mouth begin to water. That night when he first saw her, he'd felt her presence, strong for a human—especially for a woman. Then, when she pressed against him, her body and her lips on his for that brief moment of bonding....

He shook his head.

Tori could never know. If she knew what he'd done, even if it was to save her life, she'd never forgive him. No. She'd try to kill him again, and this time she might actually succeed.

Still, one more bite and their bond would be complete. *Dominatore* and *compagna* for eternity. He could do it, even without her consent, but she'd never truly be his that way. And even that bond could be broken with enough stubbornness. If there was one thing that girl had in excess, it was stubbornness.

* * * *

Tori popped one of the little white pills into her mouth and gulped down a bit of water. Without the little darlings, she'd never sleep a wink.

She flicked on the nightstand radio so that the sound of classical music filled the room. She didn't know much about Mozart and the others, but it helped her sleep. So did the list she mentally checked off every night. The windows and doors were locked; the cell phone was on the nightstand. Security system was armed. Her bedroom door blocked out enough light to give her a bit of security while still allowing her to hear if someone came in or walked down the hallway. Everything done—except the hall light.

If there wasn't a light on in the hall, she'd never sleep. Sometimes those shadows grew too close and noises woke her to darkness that seemed to move and breathe. She moved to the hall, checked to make sure nothing was there, then darted to the bathroom door and reached her arm around to flip on the light. She padded back to her room, snuggled back in, and reached over to flick off the lamp.

When she snuggled into the bed, she curled one leg over her body pillow and her free hand checked the gun under her pillow. A girl couldn't be too careful, especially when the monsters knew who she was and that she had no protector. Of course, the fact that she'd almost killed Michael in front of a crowd didn't hurt, either. No one had to know it was an accident.

He was the most intimidating *vampiro* in town, not to mention one of the hottest. In fact, if he were human, she'd have done him a long time ago. There was just something about being dead that made a guy less attractive. One vampire boyfriend in a lifetime was plenty, especially if the first one tried to kill you and the potential second was a blood-sucking Casanova.

Chapter Three

TORI LAY in the bed with her eyes closed, trying to drift off to sleep, but every time she tried, her mind went back to Michael's mouth on hers. She wanted him more than she should.

Her body throbbed with the memory of his mouth on her neck. She reached a hand down between her legs and slid it slowly over the front of her panties. The image of him bending to her neck flashed behind her eyelids and brought a quake from her toes to her head.

She pulled her hand back. She wasn't going to do this, not about him.

The aching skin between her legs protested and Tori breathed out hard. She tossed her body into the other direction and tried to think of something else. The beach. Yeah, she loved the coast. Before long, her vacation time would roll around again and she was going back to the beach. She'd find a lounge chair and recline in the sand until the sun set. Then, she'd take a walk alone in the dark, letting her feet play in the surf.

A vision of Michael catching her in his arms on that dark beach made her nipples tighten. Tori let her hand slide slowly inside the thin fabric of her panties to stroke the little button.

But, it wasn't her hand she was imagining. In her mind, Michael stroked her along and whispered indecent words in her ear.

It didn't take long to bring the spasm that had her panting and soaked.

* * * *

Tori's eyes opened when she heard someone come in. The room was a large expanse of marble with gold and crimson draperies, art, and statues. Candles lit the room from several directions, as did ancient oil lamps. It looked like something straight out of that movie she'd watched about the Spartan King Leonidas and his three hundred warriors. When she'd fallen asleep, she was in her bed. So unless someone had managed to sneak her to ancient Rome, surely this was a dream.

A woman cleared her throat near the door. She was dressed in a tan robe and her hair was bound in an intricate design. Although Tori knew that she'd never seen the woman before, she had all the familiarity of a family member. But, that was how dreams worked. The mind didn't question people who it knew should be there because it put them there.

The woman motioned upward. She said something, but it was in another language. Still, Tori knew what she meant somehow. The petite dark-haired woman wanted her to move forward, to allow them to prepare her.

Tori slipped off the bed. Something hit her knees and she looked down to see that she too wore a long linen toga, but hers was crimson with gold edging. Instinct told her that this was a disgraceful dress for a woman and it brought to mind prostitution. Great, so she was a hooker in ancient Rome.

She stepped forward and raised her arms as the woman slipped a gold bracelet on each arm. The woman inserted dangling earrings into Tori's ears, and then dabbed at her with a stick of something that looked like charcoal. "Close your eyes."

She closed her eyes and allowed her to paint dark lines on her face. The woman brushed something red on her lips that tasted strange and burned a little.

She pushed Tori to sit and went to work on her hair. More dangling things went in her hair, which was twisted to resemble snakes falling around her face. Her head felt heavy, and the sheer cloth that was draped over her head and shoulders expounded the feeling. There was no mirror, but she imagined how exotic she must look.

"Stand," she understood the woman to say. "Hold out your hands, child."

She did, and a small, soft rope wound around her wrists. She watched the woman work to tie it in an intricate knot that left a length of about four feet, which she used to pull Tori toward the door.

They walked down a long corridor and past an open courtyard that glowed in the silver light of a full moon. Two guards in sandals, tunics, leather, and metal armor spoke in hushed tones, but they stopped to watch her move past. It was definitely ancient Rome. Tori smiled at the thought. She'd been watching way too much of the History Channel.

The woman led her down a long set of stairs and through a heavy door. The inner room was dark, but moonlight spilled in through long windows that also allowed a breeze to billow the sheer curtains that draped over each. Tori couldn't see the entire area, but she knew that it was large.

When the woman spoke, her voice echoed off distant walls. "Master, we have prepared her for you."

"Thank you," Michael's voice answered in the same foreign language from the shadows a few feet in front of her and it made her heart skip a beat or two.

The woman's dainty footsteps faded away and Tori heard the door shut behind her with a loud thud.

"And you volunteered for this?"

Not really, but she would play along. It wasn't as if she dreamed about Roman vampires every day. "Yeah."

"Yes, Lord." His voice boomed and a lamp lit to her right, casting a yellowish-orange glow over a small area of the room.

Tori felt a twinge of rebellion shoot through her, but she swallowed it down. "Yes, Lord."

"Open the clasp on your top."

She held up her hands. "I can't."

Something sharp and cold hit her shoulder and then pulled at the material. She stood still, afraid of the blade. The material fell away. Her hands immediately went up to cover her bare breasts.

"Move your hands. There is no shame in your nakedness."

Her arms held their place.

"I said, move your hands." Michael nudged the ropes a little with the blade. "I will not warn you again."

She let her arms fall away slowly.

"Do you know why you're here?"

"Not exactly."

"You are to serve me."

"In what way?" After the words came out, she felt the sting of embarrassment. No doubt, she was here for his sexual pleasure. This was, after all, a dream and she was beginning to enjoy it.

"In whatever way I choose." He stepped close enough for her to feel the heat from his body, and she could finally see him. He was dressed in a white toga and his face was much the same as in life, but with more expression. He looked human, even though she'd never realized that he hadn't looked that way every other time she'd seen him.

Michael's hand slid up her arm and her skin erupted in chills. The fingers lingered over her collarbone and then slipped down the cleft between her breasts. When his hand cupped her breast, Tori heard a hiss of air leave his lips. He stroked her softly, lingering on the curved underside, and then let his fingers play over her nipple. They hardened for him and a shameless smile parted his lips. "You are magnificent."

He palmed her swollen nipple and then grabbed it between his thumb and forefinger. The little squeeze brought a shot of pain and a surprising purr from her parted lips. "Do you enjoy pain?"

"No."

"Then I will try to be gentle." He squeezed the nipple again and the feeling went straight to her clit, making it throb in time with her heartbeat. "At least until you are accustomed to my needs."

His mouth landed on hers. When their lips met, they replayed the kiss they'd shared in the club. This time, since it was a dream, Tori leaned into it and matched his force. She opened to let his tongue slide over hers. Michael's hand dropped the length of guide rope and went to her waist. He probed her mouth with his tongue and moaned when she nipped it with her teeth.

Tori brushed the back of her hand over him and felt his solid bare abdomen, then the waistband of his robe, and below that—his massive erection. She pressed the back of her hand against it while his mouth ran down her chin in a series of hot kisses. Michael moaned. She turned her hand and fondled him lazily until he began to push against her in a slow rhythm.

When his mouth went to the scar on her neck, she pulled back a little. Dream or no dream, she wasn't letting a vampire bite her.

He caught her quickly and gave her a ferocious look, the kind that a dog gives when you take away his favorite bone. "Don't pull away from me." Michael's hands hooked her waist firmly. He pressed forward, forcing her back a few paces until she ran into a column that she hadn't known was behind her. "You are mine, and nothing I do here is for anything less than our ultimate pleasure. Because of that, you will bend to my will."

Michael pushed her bound hands over her head, then moved his mouth to her chest. His teeth scraped over her skin. "Understood?"

Her heart thundered in her chest. The strength in his words, the force in his touch—all of the things she would have slapped him for in real life—were erotic here, where there was no one to judge her. So, she nodded and let her arms fall down around his head. She arched her neck toward his mouth. "Yes."

"Do you submit to me, Victoria?" In a moment, she felt his teeth scratch across the scar tissue from Robert's attack.

"Yessss."

"Open for me," he whispered against her skin while his hands worked up the skirt of her robe.

Tori parted her legs, then gasped when his hand went between them. One strong finger slid across her flesh. It pumped slowly at first, then sped up, while his thumb stroked her clit in careful but firm motions.

When her knees threatened to give way, Michael caught her hips. He pulled her straight up, pinning her to the cold stone column with powerful hands, then pushed his hips forward so that his tip pressed against her soaked flesh.

In a slow impalement, he penetrated her with his warm length. Tori moaned, drawing his eyes up to hers. She stared into them as he thrust deeper. It was like staring into the face of a man fighting back his demons. Such struggle, and yet, such control.

When his eyes glanced at her throat, she arched her neck and used her hands to prompt him forward. He resisted, then let himself fall into the bend of her neck. First, she felt his breath and caught that familiar scent of him. His mouth clamped on her flesh, and his teeth pushed into her skin with a popping sound that made her wince. She breathed deeply and felt her mind relax into the magic of his bite. Then, she went into that heavenly place again where they were one body, joined at the hips, and sharing the frantic beat of her heart as he drew the life's blood from her neck. She drifted into a blissful world where the only thing that mattered was the orgasms ripping through her body—and that it was Michael who brought them.

Chapter Four

IN THE back corner booth of Bruno's Diner, Tori yanked her hair back in a ponytail with a black band that matched her monochrome sweats. The cell phone rested between her head and shoulder, listening to the Muzak that played from the other line, competing for her attention with the Tim McGraw song coming from the jukebox in the back corner of the diner near the restrooms.

As she lowered her arms, she caught a whiff of something. She stopped and looked at her forearm, then casually sniffed her skin. It was him. Michael. The smell of him was on her skin, even though she'd taken a bath after seeing him. She let out a snort and wiped her hand on her pants.

"Sorry." Danny's voice came back on the line. "Now, what's this about you and Michael? Are you letting him feed on you, too?"

"Danny, I really don't see where it's any of your business." She lifted the large cup to her lips, sipped the hot chocolate, and then set the cup back on the table.

"You're putting your neck out to find this killer, and with *him* no less." Danny grunted on the other end of the line. "It's a bad idea."

"What else am I gonna do? You want me to walk into *The Scene* by myself?"

"No. You know that's not what I meant." Tori could hear Danny clicking a pen on the other end as he continued. "Just let them handle their own. It's better that way. For all of us."

"I can't. I have to make it official. My job's counting on it."

"What about Jonas? Couldn't he take you in?"

"Probably, but I think I'd be even more at risk." Tori sipped her drink again, careful not to scorch her tongue.

"Why?"

"Jonas doesn't get the kind of respect Michael does."

He laughed. "Exactly. And how do you think Michael got that respect, Tori? It's not from helping the homeless. He's a monster and you know it."

She sighed. "But I still can't do it without him. He's the only chance I've got of making it out of that place unmarked."

"Every human in this city who knows about vampires has a master. Without one, you're asking to get hurt."

"And with one, I'm a slave."

"I resent that. Alana loves me."

"Okay, Danny, but you've gotta admit the obvious."

"What's that?"

"If she decided to make you do something, there's not a thing you could do to stop her."

"But she wouldn't."

"I know, but humor me."

Danny let out a long breath. "Okay. You're right. So the fuck what?"

Tori smiled in triumph. "Yeah, I don't ever want to risk being under anyone's control like that."

"You know it's bound to happen sooner or later. If you don't pick a master to align yourself with, then some nut's gonna pick for you."

"I know, but I can't do it, yet."

"Just be careful. A lot of these guys would love to have you as a servant. You come with great connections."

She glanced at the clock. "I've got to go."

"Call me if you need me."

"Will do."

There was a click on the other end of the line. Danny never said goodbye. It might have been that he was sentimental that way, but she suspected that it was mostly because he was always in a hurry. He loved his job as a paramedic, but sometimes he didn't stop long enough to sleep.

Tori set the phone down and glanced into the brown shopping bag beside her. The pile of black leather didn't look any less strange than it had in the store, but somehow it seemed less threatening the more she looked at it. Maybe, if she looked at it a lot before sundown, she would even be comfortable enough to wear it to Michael's. Not that she really had a choice.

* * * *

On a small, black leather couch in the *vampiro's* private bar, Michael sat with his arm hooked around Jessica's shoulders. Or maybe she was Jill. He had a hard time keeping the twins straight, and to be honest, they annoyed him more than a little, but they were healthy, easily manipulated, and they donated blood freely.

She leaned closer so that her perfume filled his nostrils, and whispered. "Vlad's coming this way. He looks mad."

"I need to talk to you, Michael."

He glanced up to see Jonas standing in front of them. He wasn't in stage clothes, which is what he always wore in the club. Instead, he was wearing what he'd been wearing downstairs. Just a pair of worn jeans and white socks. Michael arched a brow. "Does this need to be private?"

The man nodded and moved quickly toward the back.

Michael hesitated, then slipped from the booth to follow him.

"Are you coming back?" Jessi-Jill asked, faking a pout.

"Probably."

She twisted her finger in her hair. "Promise or I'll start looking for someone else while you're gone."

Michael shrugged. "Be my guest."

Before she huffed, he turned and weaved through the crowd to the private room off the north wall. Michael stepped inside to a dark room with red light that gave Jonas' pale skin a strange glow. With the black leather couch in the corner behind him and Goth posters on the wall, he looked strangely out of his element.

Michael shut the door. "What is it?"

"You can't help Victoria."

Michael stared at him for a long moment. He was admittedly shocked by the lower-ranking male's sudden arrogance, but more so by his matter-of-fact tone. "Why?"

"She doesn't trust us. And we can't trust her."

He knew this was coming, but he hadn't expected Jonas to be the one. So, he crossed the room, shaking his head. At the couch, he turned and sat on the edge. He folded his hands in front of him. "She's a human. If she tries anything, we will know."

"You always underestimate her." Jonas moved to stand in front of him, his arms crossed in front of his chest. "Like when she tried to kill you."

His hand moved to the scar on his shoulder, the one she'd put there with three bullets. Never in his wildest dreams would he have imagined that woman attacking him. She had the heart of a warrior, that one. So, yeah she was a bit unpredictable. But that was her best quality. She was a force to be reckoned with.

Jonas smirked. "I know what you're thinking—she's not a toy, Michael."

"I know that." He smiled. "But, she will be an interesting *compagna*."

"She's not your mate, either."

He couldn't help but grin. "She will be."

"No. She won't. Don't you get it?" Jonas threw up his hands. "She'll get us all killed, especially if you go after Damon. It's the same thing as before. You couldn't control yourself when they killed Elizabeth, and that landed us with Castillo. Now, he'll have all of our heads because you couldn't resist another fu—"

"Enough!" Michael was suddenly on his feet and Jonas jumped back instinctually. Anger bubbled up inside him, along with a strange need to protect her. Jonas was right, but something in the bond that he shared with Tori overrode his sense.

"You'd fight me over this? Don't you see what she does to you?"

His face was more pleading than Michael had seen it in decades. Jonas was too scared to help them work this plan. He'd have to be eased into the idea or he'd blow the entire deal.

Michael let out a breath and moved closer. His hand reached up slowly to pat Jonas on the shoulder. "You've made your point, *fratello*. Perhaps I am a little drunk with the idea of her. You understand how it is."

"No." His eyes locked on Michael's. "No human female has ever had this effect on me."

"No. But, I do recall a certain *sorella* who had you on hands and knees in Rome."

Jonas chuckled. "That was different."

"Really?"

Jonas stared into his eyes for a moment. "She was one of us, Michael."

"Does it make that much of a difference? We were all human at one time."

"Yeah, but we can't have a human around the *cosca*. It won't work. The *sorella* will kill her."

Michael stopped, his hands fought to clench, but he took a long breath. "They won't go against my word."

"You're probably right." Jonas clapped a hand on Michael's shoulder. "You are my brother. I want this for you, but you must remember that Alana has almost as much power as we do because Danny is her mate. Another human. Without you being *padrone*, if you take a human, we don't have enough strength to stop the other families if they tried to take over. You need a real mate—soon."

Michael let the tension flow out of his body. "You are sworn to secrecy, as always."

Jonas nodded. "Of course."

"Victoria is no ordinary human. She knows nothing of her own abilities, but I sensed them when we bonded. She has power in her blood, like the old witches."

"But she doesn't use it?"

"I don't think she knows it's there."

"And you can tap into it."

Michael nodded.

A wicked grin crept across Jonas' face. "So, you are thinking with your brain after all."

Michael laughed and gave him a strong but playful slap on the arm. "You have to learn to trust me."

* * * *

Tori took as deep a breath as she could in the black leather corset and tried to look confident. She strode toward the bouncers, ignoring the line that formed along the sidewalk. If she were going to pretend to be Michael's lover, there was no way she was standing in line to get in. Besides, who'd believe she had to?

"Whoa!" Gregory the bouncer gave her a devilish smirk. "I think I saw you in a wet dream once."

"Can it, Greg." She slipped between them and headed for the door.

"Hey, you can't do that."

She heard him moving up behind her as she grabbed the handle. "Watch me."

She tugged on the door, but Blane caught the handle. When she looked up, he smiled down and nodded once. "Jonas told me to let you come and go as you please."

"Thanks."

He leaned closer. "Between us, I always knew you two would get together. Michael needs a *shiava* like you. Someone real."

She wanted to argue, but choked down the fact that he'd practically just called her Michael's new lover. Still, he did give her kudos for being a real person instead of a bimbo. Maybe Blane wasn't so bad. "Congratulations. You just made it on my Christmas card list."

He laughed and pulled the door open for her. "I'll be looking forward to that."

She walked inside, again bombarded by music, and bypassed the coat check. No way were they taking her gun now, during an investigation where she was undercover as a vampire's sidekick.

"Good evening, Victoria." Jonas' deep voice rolled up her arm, over her shoulder, then tickled her neck.

She glanced right.

He sat in a corner booth with a suggestive grin stretching across his face. He was messing with her mind again, damn it. Jonas was the resident rock star for a reason, all hot body and sex appeal. Even the black wife-beater shirt he was wearing, the one that showed the ancient looking tattoo running around his upper arm, seemed a perfectly planned se-duction device. His blatant arrogance annoyed the hell out of her. But, when he smiled and motioned her toward the seat beside him, she took a steadying breath and moved to-ward him, hoping that he couldn't sense exactly how hot she thought he was. And, if he tried to roll her again this time, Michael had better do something about it. "Evening, Jo—uh—Vlad."

"Join me for a drink?"

"Where's Michael?"

"He is busy at the moment. So, he asked me to keep you company." He took a sip from a tall glass of red liquid. It looked like a daiquiri, but she knew it wouldn't be. They didn't eat or drink regular food unless it was mixed with blood.

She slid into the seat opposite him. "What's he doing?"

"Having dinner."

Tori's heart dropped to her stomach. She knew he fed off other women, but she'd never gotten used to that fact. Though she had no claim over him, she'd never quite been able to stomach the idea of some strange woman wrapped in his arms and giving herself to him in every way possible. The dream only made it worse.

Jonas' eyes went to her mouth, then her neck. He didn't stare, but something in the casual glance made her rub her neck absently.

She swallowed hard and realized that she'd zoned out. "Sorry I asked."

Jonas laughed and the sound made the hair on her arms stand at attention. "I see you're no more comfortable with us than you were before."

She shrugged.

"It doesn't surprise me. You're not like the others. You don't enjoy what we do. I don't see you getting excited by the idea of me putting you on the rack."

"Amen to that." When he laughed a second time, she shivered and said, "Stop doing that."

"Why?"

"It's creepy."

"Only because you're fighting it."

She quirked a brow at him. "What is it supposed to do?"

Jonas wiggled his brows.

"Geez." She rolled her eyes.

"Can't blame me for trying. Usually you cover everything. Tonight though, you look very—uh—appealing. It suits you."

"Thanks. I think." She folded her arms in front of her waist.

"Question." Jonas took a sip of his drink.

"Knock yourself out."

"Why did you try to kill Michael the last time you were here?"

She let out a deep breath. Of all the things to ask. "It's a long story."

"I've got time."

"Okay. How about, it's none of your business."

"Yes, it is. I'm his second and I have to protect him. If you tried to kill him once, you might try again."

"I won't."

"But, how do I know?"

"Because I said so."

"That counts for nothing. Now, tell me why."

She groaned. "I walked in on him—uh—eating."

"Ah."

"Why ah?"

"I knew about your past, but I couldn't figure out what would make you so angry that you'd do that in public and risk the *Alleanza*. Or even why he didn't just wipe your memory." He took another sip. "I guess he didn't have time."

"Nope."

"You think we're all just waiting to kill you, don't you?"

She shrugged.

"We're not. Your fiancé was a mistake. Some of us would like to do much nicer things to your body." He ran his tongue slowly over a fang. "He should never have been turned."

She glanced away, trying not to see his tongue in her mind. "Not that I don't agree. But why do you say that?"

"The change magnifies our personalities. Sometimes, especially when the *creatore* has mental issues, the *neonato* loses control of their strongest deviations and desires. If he had to be done, Olivia should have taken him elsewhere for his *prova*."

Tori glared at him before she could stop herself. "Don't mention that name to me."

"Why?"

"He was cheating on me with her."

"Oh." He drained the remainder of the glass. "I suppose I should have realized that it was a bad subject. I didn't know you then, but now I just can't see you sharing your fiancé."

"I wouldn't."

He shrugged. "He was a fucking prick anyway."

"Jonas!"

"Well, he was."

Tori nodded. Jonas was right and even she couldn't deny it. She had loved Robert, or at least she'd thought she did. But, now she was beginning to wonder if it hadn't been some sick need to replace her father. He really hadn't been loving. Obsessed with her was more like it.

Jonas slid toward the end of the booth. "Michael calls."

"Damn, that's creepy. I don't know how you guys live with all of those voices floating around in your heads. It's disturbing."

He laughed again and this time it held no magic. It was just a regular, masculine chuckle. A comforting one that made her smile.

Chapter Five

TORI STOOD back a few feet from Jonas. He was humming a fast-paced song and wore a sensual cologne that wafted her way. She didn't move closer to him. Instead, she tried to keep an eye on the door at the end of the black painted hallway. No sense in letting vampires sneak up on them in the hallway. They were his friends. Not hers.

Jonas opened the door and motioned her inside. "Let's go."

She stepped into a room painted entirely in flat black; he'd redecorated since the night she shot him. The painted silhouette of a church steeple on the wall behind Michael's chrome desk was in a lighter shade of black. To the right was a sitting area with an oversized black couch and chairs huddled around a small glass *koi* pond and waterfall that ran up the wall. Ornate kimonos hung on the walls with special lighting shining on their glass chambers. Silk brocade curtains hung over windows that showed a realistic *trompe l'oeil* of the Tokyo skyline, complete with tiny lights. Only Michael could pull off a room like that without seeming eccentric.

"He'll be here soon."

Tori nodded and moved toward a curio cabinet that housed what appeared to be antique weapons. She tugged on the door and it rattled, but didn't move, so she moved on to the pond. She knelt beside it and watched two smaller fish swimming around the bottom like they were playing tag. Then, a curious white and orange fish swam to the surface, but when she touched its flowing fin with her finger, it darted away.

"Jonas, please go check in on Emma." Michael's voice pulled her to her feet and she turned to see him moving toward his desk in a black business suit. "I'm afraid she took her human companion and Damon to her chamber."

He nodded and left the room so fast that the closing of the door sent a short burst of wind across Tori.

She watched Michael slip off the jacket, place it on a hook behind him, and then shuffle through papers on the desk without so much as nod in her direction. She rubbed her arm casually to warm her skin. With the door closed, the room felt colder, and she wasn't sure if it was the temperature.

"Please, sit." Michael clicked a remote that made a cyclone of fire burst to life in a column that jutted out from the wall.

At least he had noticed she was cold. She moved to the large chair closest to the fireplace and sat, watching him glide toward the couch across from her. "Nice office."

"Thank you." He slid onto the couch and leaned back. His legs fell into that normal guy position and he draped one arm across the back. "I am already being questioned about our relationship. No one believes it. So, for this scheme of ours to work, everyone must believe that you are my lover. They must see you in my office, in my arms, and at my side."

Something in the way he said the word made her face flush. She glanced toward the fire.

"Are you still confident in your acting abilities?"

"Sure." She glanced back and he gave her a sly smile. He'd noticed.

She glanced down, away from his eyes, and saw a spot of red next to his tie. She smiled. "Um—Michael, you spilled your dinner."

His eyes darted down quickly and he pushed the tie in front of the spot. His cheeks seemed a tinge pinker than usual. She smiled to herself. *Point for the human.*

Michael settled back into his normal vampire façade and she couldn't read his expression. "I've been thinking about it and there's no way you can convince Castillo long enough to even get into *The Scene* without at least a little knowledge about the lifestyle."

"Okay."

"Tonight will be a trial run. Ask anything you need to and then we're going to go into the real club to see if you can convince my *cosca.*"

"Okay, then I've got a few questions about bondage, since they're all apparently into that sort of thing."

"Alright, ask."

"Why do you enjoy this?"

He laughed. "If these are going to be personal questions, then I believe I have the right to ask a few in return."

"They're not personal."

"Aren't you asking about *my* preferences and choices?"

She hated it when he was right. "Okay."

"You agree, then?"

"Yes."

"Then, to answer your question, I enjoy giving others what they most desire but are too ashamed to ask for." He grinned. "Why are you so uptight?"

She groaned. "I'm not uptight."

"Yes, you are."

"I—I don't know, then."

"Yes, you do. You resist any form of pleasure."

"Like what?"

"Your attraction to me."

"I am—" He raised his brows in protest. *Dammit.* "I don't know."

"Fair enough, next question."

"What made it a turn-on to beat someone during sex? Did you have a traumatic childhood?"

He looked thoughtful and the vampire mask seemed to slide away while his brows knitted. Then, his face went blank again. "No."

"You're lying."

He sighed. "I suppose you could say that I did have a traumatic childhood."

"How?"

"You've already had your question." He gave her an emotionless smile. "Do you like to be bitten during sex?"

"What?"

He didn't repeat the question.

Tori shifted in her seat. "I'm not answering that."

"Then you do."

"I didn't say that."

"I can hear your heart racing, Victoria."

She groaned again. "Fuck. Alright! Yeah." She leaned forward to rest her elbows on her knees. She needed something good to ask him. Something to make him squirm. "What is more stimulating for you, pain or sexual pleasure?"

"Both. Together."

"I do not understand that."

"Yes, you do." He leaned forward to match her posture. "More than you'd like to admit." He stared at her, searching her eyes for a response, which made her look away. "How long has it been since a man gave you what you wanted, Victoria?"

Her eyes snapped back to him. "That's too personal."

"We set no limits on the questions. Answer me."

"Robert was the last."

"That was two years ago." He leaned back. "There is no chance that your *boy* could have known what you wanted. He was an imbecile. I meant a man, someone who knew your deepest desires."

"I'm not answering this question. It's ridiculous." Tori stood. "You already have my answer."

He stood and moved to her so fast that she didn't quite see it.

Tori stumbled away, trying to put distance between them, but something hit the back of her leg. When she started to go down, he caught her by the upper arms.

Michael pulled her onto her feet, staring down at her with mischief in his eyes. His voice was soft, almost a whisper. "Someone should have taken you by now."

That place deep down where his fingers had been in the dream began to throb. Suddenly, she was aware of just how good he smelled again. All spicy and male. And how warm his skin was. But, that was because he'd been feeding. On some other woman.

Tori anchored her feet and tried to pull back, but Michael held her tight, close to his body. "I'm not that easy to get away from, Detective."

Her heart leapt into her throat and she snaked a hand up to try to use his chest for leverage. It was firm and inviting, with muscle rippling beneath the businesslike exterior. If he'd been human, she would bet that he worked out. Men just didn't have muscles like that without a lot of work.

God, it had been too long. A monster had her by the arms and she was checking out his pecs.

She shook her head to try to clear her mind, but he leaned closer. His nose came close to her cheek and he took a long whiff of her hair. He let out a long, growling approval that made the tiny hairs on her neck stand straight. She let out a yelp.

"I smell it." He leaned back enough for her to see his eyes clouding. He whispered in a growling tone, "The fear. The need. And just how much I turn you on."

His voice snapped her back. She jerked one arm up, breaking his thumb's grip, turned to put a little distance between them, and then used her right hand to land a hard slap across his cheek. "Back off!"

His head rocked, but his grip held her tight, and his body curled in. A trickle of blood oozed out the corner of his mouth and slithered down to his chin. A wicked grin made him suddenly look monstrous. "You're making it very difficult for me to restrain myself."

"Well, do a better fucking job."

She shoved him hard with her free hand, but he didn't budge. Instead, he grabbed her upper arm again and pulled her into a hard kiss. The harder she struggled, the more intense the kiss grew until his free hand slipped up to the dip in her back and stroked the leather. With the hand came warmth that spread up her spine to tickle her brain.

Something inside her screamed to run, but his lips were soft and skillful. Instead, Tori grabbed his shoulder and melted into the kiss. Her tongue snaked over his and the taste of his blood tingled on her tongue. She shivered and he pulled her harder against him, molding their bodies so that she could feel him hard against her belly.

It made her pull away from his mouth and pant. "I can't do this with y—"

His mouth was back on hers.

She faltered for a moment, letting him kiss her again before she pulled back once more. She jerked through his grip as fast as she could, throwing herself away from him. Even though she stumbled, she managed to keep her footing and start away from him.

He grunted, "Stop fighting this."

Tori struggled to breathe through the arousal and paced toward his desk to stop the throbbing between her legs. God, she wanted him. Maybe it was just because she was lonely and maybe it was more mind tricks, but she couldn't stop herself. If she let it go any further, he'd become her addiction.

When she reached the desk, she turned to find him staring down at her with hungry eyes. She glanced behind her, then back to him. Damn, he moved fast.

"This ends right now. You have been pushing me away for too long with foolish justifications." He caught her neck in both hands and stroked his thumb over her cheek as his eyes looked into hers. Her nipples ached and it was all she could do not to reach for him. "I'm not one of your boys, Victoria. I won't play this game."

The moment she relented, something broke free in her mind. She gasped and her heart pounded in her ears. Lust washed over her like some sinful magic that she had pent up for too long. She wasn't sure if it was hers or his, but she didn't have time to think before her mind went blood-red. "Are you doing this, Michael?"

"No." Michael pulled her toward him. "You are." When their lips met, heat flooded through her body. Her senses numbed with it as he moved them back until her body pressed against the edge of his desk. Then he lifted her up to sit.

His mouth moved down the line of her jaw, while his hands reached for her legs. He pushed the skirt up, stopping at the gun and holster on her thigh. "I knew you had one somewhere."

She smiled and gripped his shoulder as he shoved the skirt over it. He pressed his body into the space between them, grinding his zipper against the lace that separated them and his mouth took her neck in covetous kisses that sent tremors through her body. He found her pulse and bit softly. With each nibble, she moaned. Each time, he responded with a groan and scratched his teeth across her skin again, as if it were as much a turn-on for him as it was her.

She grabbed his waistband and opened his pants. Inside, she wrapped her hand around his hard length. She slid down to the base of his shaft, up the length of him, and over the head in a slow movement that left her palm wet. She squeezed once and felt his canines lengthen against her neck. The sensation made her body shake.

Michael's mouth caught hers in a slow, wet kiss. His hands captured her wrists, then pulled them behind her. With one hand, he held them firmly but comfortably in place. The other stroked the top mound of flesh pressed into place by her corset, which wasn't any looser than when they'd started. He watched her eyes as he snaked his hand down her side, to her hip, and then in between her legs. His hand wrapped in the lace on one hip and yanked it apart, then repeated on the other side. He tossed the ripped panties aside.

"Wait," Tori said.

"What?"

"Condom?"

Michael grunted. "I can't carry disease and I can't get you pregnant."

When she nodded, he pushed his hips forward, spreading her legs farther apart, until their bodies touched. Tori gasped and let her eyes close. She felt a jolt of pleasure just before Michael used his free hand to hold her hip and push himself inside her.

He made several thrusts, each bringing a groan from his lips, forcing her body to accept him. A long moan rolled out as her lips parted. Her eyes closed again. Her legs hooked over his hips, and he ground deeper. She tugged her arms to grasp his shoulders and Michael let out a small growl. Then he pushed again until their hips met.

When she leaned her head back and took a long breath, his mouth went to her neck. Alarms went off in her mind, but her neck arched toward him anyway, as if she'd lost all control of her body. Maybe she did want him to bite her. Every part of her body was electric. It wasn't human sex, by any stretch of the imagination. No, something was making his every gesture even more exotic, like they were caught in some sort of gluttonous magic. Maybe—

Before she could finish the thought, he thrust against her again. His hips worked in a firm pace that pushed her almost to the brink. Teeth scraped the surface of her skin and sent a shot of pain up her neck that flared and throbbed. The longing for him to take her neck weighed so hard that it threatened to drown her. She'd thought about him taking her for years, imagined being the woman in his bed. Fuck what everyone else thought.

She whimpered. "Do it, Michael."

He let out a deep moan and replaced the teeth with lips that sucked hard on her skin.

"Please. Bite me."

"No." His voice was almost a growl. When his mouth closed over the scratch again, he sucked harder.

She tugged to try to free her arms as he pulled another moan from her lips. A wave of tension rolled through her. She was almost there. "Please."

Michael's free hand looped in her hair, then jerked her head back and to the side. The two tiny points pressed hard against her jugular, but didn't penetrate. Then, his tongue made a sweep across her skin and licked across her pulse, while his hips thrust against her.

Tori's body shuddered against him, a spasm from behind her navel. She heard herself moaning loudly, but her mind floated in an orgasmic high that she never knew existed. It wasn't natural, or human. In the illusion, she felt Michael's

power rolling around her like a stiff wind. They were one being, safe in this space. Their space.

Then, she felt Michael's control slipping as clearly as if
it were her own. The wind whipped too hard. She fell from
that orgasmic subspace, back into her physical form, crash-
ing into a panting female body that lay locked in the steel
grip of a man.

His forehead pressed against hers and it was the first time
she'd ever heard him catch his breath.

"Michael." She opened her eyes to see his closed lids.
"What was that?"

He leaned back enough to smile at her and then gave her a
soft kiss. His hand released her wrists. She wiggled her arms
a little to relieve the stiffness while his fingers gripped her
sides. He kissed her again, a delicate caress of lips that made
her want to melt in her shoes. He pulled away and smiled
down at her. "That's what you've been missing."

Tori laughed. "Little confident?"

Someone banged on the door and Michael didn't even
glance toward it. Instead, he gave her another soft kiss.

She pulled back. "Are you going to answer that?"

"It took me this long to get you here, I'm not letting go
now to answer the door." He buried his face in her neck, nibbling softly.

She laughed just as the knock came again, harder and
faster this time. Someone cleared their throat behind the
door. Jonas' voice came next. "Michael?"

With a groan, he pulled away from her neck. Anger
flowed from him in burning waves. As he moved, the magic
seemed to crackle into a million tiny pieces and fall away.
"What is it, Jonas?"

"Trouble in Emma's room."

"Handle it." His voice was so loud and sharp that Tori
jumped.

"Uh....You really need to handle this."

"Is it an emergency?"

"Yes! I wouldn't be here if it wasn't."

He sighed and his shoulders drooped. "I am so sorry, *in-amorato*. We will finish this later." He placed a quick kiss on her lips and then turned to fix his clothes.

Tori wiped her mouth with the back of her hand and slid off the desk. She tugged her clothing into place as guilt took the places that lust had been just moments ago. One word began to loop in her mind. *Traitor*.

Tori's stomach fluttered and she shook her head. One moment she was swearing at him and the next they were actually doing it on his desk. This case was going to have to close fast.

Michael turned to give her a questioning look. His eyes focused on hers for a second before he stepped closer to the door. He opened it without saying a word to her, then spoke so quietly to Jonas that she couldn't hear.

When she glanced at them again, Michael pointed out the door. "Coming with us?"

"Sure. I want to see what exactly a vampire emergency is."

He moved out the door and she followed. Jonas held the door open for her and as she moved past, he muttered, "Well, that didn't take long."

"Fuck you, Jonas."

"Problem?" Michael held the elevator door open and watched them.

"No." She sped up and slipped in beside him.

She blinked to see Jonas standing suddenly next to her. The vampire tricks were getting far too creepy. They didn't usually show off this much—or maybe they'd been hiding it all along, toning down their natural behavior for her benefit?

She glanced at each of them, suddenly aware of the fact that they were descending into a tomb and that she was the only one breathing. There was absolutely no movement, other than her own, and the mechanical sounds of the elevator as it lowered, then stopped.

Cries ripped through the room as the elevator doors slid open. The guys were gone in a blink. From the sound of footsteps, she knew where they'd headed. She ran out behind them and followed the curve of the stone hallway.

"I said to get the fuck out, Damon." Michael's voice took a tone that she'd never heard before. And the last word—the name Damon—sounded more like a hiss.

She rounded a corner and saw a young man slide out the door on his back. He stopped just in front of her feet. She managed not to fall on him, but stumbled over him instead. When she looked back, he smiled up at her. It made her skin crawl.

"Hello, love." His Scottish accent echoed through the corridor.

Before she could respond, he was standing, crowding her up against the wall as he straightened his shirt. "And whose pet are you?"

The man's hand went for her chest, or her arm; she wasn't sure which because another hand stopped it. Michael was beside her so fast that it made her jump. She banged her head against the wall and grabbed it quickly, trying to rub away the flower-burst of pain in her skull. "Shit."

"She's mine, Damon." The electricity in the air rose so that the hair on her arms stood again.

"Oh, but the *cane* would look so nice hanging from my ceiling." Damon eased into an evil grin that reminded her of the Joker. "I bet she has a beautiful scream."

"The only ceiling she'll be hanging from is mine." Michael was right up in Damon's face, his own face twisting in a snarl.

The man made a tsk, tsk sound. "Michael, when will you learn to share with your *fratello*?"

"You are not one of us. You wouldn't have survived the *prova* if it weren't for Castillo."

He smirked. "I may not be as strong as you, but if I ask for her as my *shiava* it will happen."

Michael wrenched the man's wrist.

"Don't try me, Michael. I smell you on her, but she is still a *senza vincolo*. If you have no mark on her, she is illegal and I can take her by law."

"You shouldn't make huge fucking assumptions." Veins were bulging in Michael's temples as he squeezed the arm a little harder, making bones crack loud enough for Tori to hear. "We were finishing her *vincolo* when you interrupted me."

Damon jerked his hand away and gave her a wink. "When you tire of Michael's old ways, I will gladly take you."

Tori grabbed Michael's hand. "No, thanks."

Damon bowed to her quickly and disappeared. The ding of the elevator door as it opened was the only sound of his leaving. Spooky.

Michael pulled her close and whispered. "I saw his thoughts. He is the one and he was imagining doing it to you." He kissed her cheek and squeezed her once. "But he'd have to go through me first."

She smiled and her heart warmed. What was the world coming to? The idea of a vampire boyfriend was starting to sound good.

Jonas' voice echoed through the corridor. "I can't find her. I can't find the human."

He sounded panicked, so she stepped away. Michael moved into the room and she followed. Emma, the petite brunette that Jonas sometimes used in his act, sat on a disheveled bed. She was wrapped in a purple satin robe, nursing an eye that was well on its way to black. Around her, the room's walls displayed photos of bound women that matched the black straps on the device hanging from the ceiling in the corner. On the headboard, cuffs were built into place. Being alone in this room with Damon would have been hell.

While the guys searched the closet and under the bed, Tori moved to the bathroom. It was empty. Then a sound caught her attention. A moan.

She opened the bathroom closet door. Inside was a shivering, mumbling young blonde with whip and bite marks crisscrossing her breasts. Not fang bites, but the kind that psychos give you when they want your flesh to give for them. She lay on the stone floor, wrapped in a bloodstained sheet. Her hair lay in locks of sweat and blood, and wounds from what looked like a whip covered her back. "Oh. Uh… guys, I think she's in shock."

Tori knelt beside her to get a good look. She was barely old enough to get into the club. "Miss?"

The woman groaned.

Jonas appeared beside her. "We sent Damon back to his master. You're safe, sweetheart."

Michael appeared, too. "If you won't watch, then go. Otherwise, you can never speak of what you see here."

She nodded.

He reached for the girl and she screamed, sliding as far into the corner as she could. Michael reached out again, slower this time. "I won't hurt you. Just look at me."

When she did, her face went slack and her pupils dilated. Was this how it looked when they did the *affascinare*?

He scooted closer to her. Then, Michael slit his wrist with a fang and when the blood began to run, he pushed it to her mouth. The girl latched on greedily, but after a few slurps, he pulled away. After a few long moments, he sat her solidly on the floor again, where she began to wipe her mouth and lick her fingers. "Jonas, take her home and send her roses tomorrow from Emma."

Jonas nodded. He knelt beside them and spoke to the woman in a low, calm voice with words Tori couldn't quite hear. She looked back to Michael who licked his own wrist clean. The wound stitched together quickly, making itself whole again before he lowered his arm completely to his side. A nifty trick.

Emma moved into the bathroom with them. Her eyes were trained on Jonas and her wounds began to heal already. The color once again tainted her cheeks, but she seemed to wobble a bit and didn't meet Tori's stare.

"Will she be alright?" Tori whispered.

"They'll be fine, though I think Emma may reconsider her taste for bondage after this."

"Yeah." Tori looked back at the woman again. "I think I've had enough for one night, too. I'm going home."

Michael nodded and motioned toward the door. "After you."

No one said anything to them as they left the room. They walked to the elevator in silence. Tori did glance up once to see him staring down at her. They smiled, and then entered when the doors spread open.

Inside, he pressed the button, and then turned to her. "Do you regret what happened tonight?" He took her hand and pulled her close.

His scent washed over her again and her knees weakened. This time, he seemed somehow less threatening. "No."

"Good." He gave her a rapturous kiss, but when the elevator dinged, he pulled away. "I'll see you tomorrow, then."

Chapter Six

TORI SHUFFLED through the mail as she walked in the door of her apartment. She tossed the bills onto the kitchen table and everything else went into the garbage. The smoke-colored cat jumped onto the edge.

"Get down, Blade." When she reached for him, he hissed and arched his back high. "What the—" The animal jumped down and shot toward the living room. "Don't make me wish I hadn't rescued you from that crack house, Blade."

She walked down the short hall and into the bedroom, kicking off her shoes as she went. She shimmied out of the skirt and manipulated the laces on the corset. When she finally peeled it off, she tossed it onto the bed. Tomorrow she'd have to wear something to fit in at *The Scene*. This outfit wasn't fit to burn.

She took her gun out of the thigh holster and placed it on the dresser, then grabbed the oversize tee from the bed and headed into the small bathroom. Behind her, in the hall, the floor creaked. She stopped and turned her ear toward the door slowly. The creak came again, closer this time.

"If there's someone in here, you'd better have a bazooka!"

The sound stopped.

She dropped the shirt, grabbed the pistol from its holster, pointed it, and popped the safety all in a quick, mechanical move. She crept toward the door and glanced down the dark hallway. The kitchen light was off and the area was almost black. Blade darted through the hall and into her room so fast that she let out a yelp.

She groaned and used her foot to close the door quickly, then flicked the lock. Her heart was pounding and her hand began to shake. "I have got to get a different apartment."

Tori walked back to the bathroom, grabbing the shirt on the way. She stepped inside and closed the door. After turning the lock, she placed the pistol on the shelf beside the shower and started the water. She didn't have time for this shit. She still had to get ready and meet the Chief for breakfast at six.

* * * *

Tori sat at her usual corner table at Bruno's Diner, watching people move past on the street as she sipped a cup of hot cocoa and listened to the waitress call out orders to the chef, who was filling the place with the smell of eggs, bacon, waffles, and hash browns. If she stayed longer, she'd give in and order that pecan waffle she'd been craving during that hour that Chief Ives had been late. But, what she really needed was to go home and rest before sunset.

The door dinged and she looked up to see him walk in. His tie was missing and there was a pen sticking out behind his ear. He smiled behind that walrus moustache.

"Any leads?" He slipped into the seat opposite her and grabbed a laminated menu.

"A few."

"Anything promising?"

"Yeah, actually." She took a sip and watched him watching her over the top of his menu. Life could be so much easier if he just knew about the *vampiro*. But, he didn't and there was no need to ruin his view of the world. "I think I found him."

"Who?"

"A guy we've been trying to bust for a while. A real jerk."

"Well, we've got a good line on another one. A local club owner. A real ego trip. Guy by the name of Michael."

She swallowed hard and lost track of her heartbeat in the hollow of her chest. "What kind of lead?"

"One of the officers got a tip off the flyers. Says he's running X out of a club."

She breathed again. *Good, it was probably just Damon trying to get at him.*

He perked up. "Why, you know him?"

"Yeah." She took another sip, trying to look like she had it together. "A little."

"What do you think? Could he be the guy?"

Of course, he could. If this many years of detective work had taught her one thing, it was that anyone could commit murder. Michael, as a vampire, just had more motives.

"Tyler?"

"Yeah." She set down her cup. "Uh, he could be, I guess. I doubt it though."

"Which one do you like best?"

"My guy."

"What kind of info have you got on him?"

"He's into bondage and hurting women. Some of my contacts are sure it's him and can place him near the scene."

"We'll look into both of them since you know this Michael. We're too short-staffed to try to follow both. This flu's already taken out half my team."

An aging woman in a yellow apron appeared beside the table. "What can I get ya today, Chief?"

"Double cheesy eggs, side of bacon, hash browns with everything, and a Diet Coke."

"Coming right up." The woman moved back to the counter to call the order to the cook.

"Well, I'm gone." Tori slid from her seat. "I've got another meeting with an informant this evening."

"Alright. Watch your back, Tyler. I'd feel much better about this if you'd let one of the guys go in with you."

"I'll be fine," she said, heading toward the door. She needed sleep. Lots and lots of sleep to prepare for the long night of pretending to be a vampire's slave.

* * * *

Michael stood in front of the mirror, adjusting the crimson silk tie that matched the dark suit that Tori had always liked, then stepped out of his room and into the hallway. The shirt wasn't the one he wanted to wear on his first date with Tori to *The Scene*, but it would do. The other had somehow found its way into Jonas' room and now smelled like pot and sweat, probably because he'd worn it to play a gig at a rave.

"Get him!" Jonas' voice echoed down the corridor.

The sound of Gregory and Jonas playing that game with all the machine-gunfire came before he saw them. When Michael turned the corner, he saw two grown men with controllers in hand, jumping and weaving automatically as they navigated characters on a huge plasma screen television in the parlor. Jonas, in worn jeans and a white T-shirt, leaned forward in his chair as a digital zombie came around a doorway toward his character.

"I am, dammit." Gregory, already in his uniform for the night, leaned right as his character swung a spiked baseball bat at the zombie's head.

When the head exploded, the two guys and the small audience of Jude, Blane, and Jack cheered. He'd never quite understood their affection for this game. Michael much preferred the challenge of puzzle games or those involving stealth, like that one where the object was to work as a medieval assassin. The bash and gore game didn't have the same level of challenge as the ones that required actual thought.

When the scene change screen popped up, Michael said, "Pause it."

They did, and turned toward him. Jonas smiled. "Yeah?"

"While I'm gone tonight, Jack is in charge. Blane—"

"Yeah, boss?"

"No underage girls. The last thing I need is to get busted for that."

"Okay."

"Jude, if there's any trouble, call my cell. But only call if there's an emergency."

She nodded. "Sure thing."

Michael turned to walk back to the room, but Jude spoke again. "Michael?"

"Yes?"

"You look great. She'll love it."

He smiled at her. Of all the others he had changed, Jude was probably the sweetest. He'd always hoped that time wouldn't rob her of that attribute. "Thank you."

She came closer and spoke in a hushed tone while the others resumed their game. "Are you nervous?"

"Why do you ask?"

"You're headed back to the room again to check yourself. This is the fourth time."

"Of course I'm not nervous. Just trying to make sure I get it right."

Jude put her hand on his shoulder. "You really do look nice. She'll be trying to take your clothes off on the way there."

"Not likely." He moved his shoulder from beneath her palm and moved into the bedroom.

She followed.

"She does like you. Just give her some time. Tori's trust is hard-won, but I think it must be unwavering once you have it."

He realized that he was pacing and stopped. "Perhaps."

"I've always liked her."

"You're the only one, I think."

"They'll come around. They're just afraid that she'll ruin what we have going here." She came closer and gave his arm a squeeze. "You've given us all a great home, a safe place to feel normal again. She is strong enough to withstand their tests. Let them realize that they like her on their own."

Michael nodded.

"Besides, you're the one who has the last say. We can't do anything about it if you take her."

When he looked at her, she smiled a wide smile that made the corners of his own lips turn up. "I know. I just want you all too….It's our home and I won't bring anyone in that will ruin that."

"If we accept it, it will make it easier because we won't be reminding her that she's not one of us."

"Exactly."

"I'll see what I can do, but some of it will be healthy for her. If we don't test our *padrone's* mistress, how will we know that she can be trusted? And how will she know that she can trust us? If it's too easy, Tori will not trust any of us. She knows us too well."

Michael hugged her, then gave her a soft kiss on the cheek. She stiffened, but he was glad he'd done it. Of all the progeny, Jude felt more like one of his actual children than the rest. Sometimes he even wondered if it was how a real dad felt about his daughter.

Jude giggled and pulled away. "When I snag this human doctor I've been watching, you're gonna have to do the same for me."

"Whoa. Let's not go there." Michael took her hand and moved toward the door. "One of us being mixed up with them is enough. We need to find you a nice kosher vampire."

She laughed so fully that it made him smile. "Just make sure that he has broad shoulders and dark curls. Oh, and a nice bank account."

"Is that all?" He pulled the door to his room closed behind them.

"Yeah." Jude blushed, but tried to cover it by looking away. "Let's go have a drink before she gets here. I think you need it."

He let her take his hand and lead him past the gamers toward the elevator. Watching them, he couldn't help but wonder if it would all be the same once he challenged Castillo. They were almost a real family and getting rid of the city's leader might risk more than just his life. It could mean all of their lives and he just wasn't sure that it was worth it.

* * * *

"Don't start." Tori stood at the private bar, staring at Jonas, who wore only the black PVC pants that hugged his form completely and the bracelets he kept on his right arm. His smooth chest was bare and for the first time she could see a long tattoo going down his neck that appeared to be some sort of tribal art or script, as well as the silver hoop nipple ring…not that she was looking.

"Can I at least say that you look hot?"

"You just did."

"I always imagined you in boots like that." He eyed her carefully, then wiggled his brows at her.

"Alright! That's enough." She slipped off the stool so that the heels of her black knee-high boots made a loud click.

Then she tugged down the bottom of her cropped white tee. "Just take me to Michael."

He motioned her toward a door that she'd never been through. "After you."

She grabbed her keys and cell phone from the bar and strode ahead, careful not to trip. All she needed was to sprawl out on the floor in front of everyone. Although Jonas would probably get a kick out of it.

She opened the door to a long narrow brick hallway with dim lighting. Each step she took made a click that echoed past them until the door shut behind her. Something brushed past her. Jonas was in front of her so fast that she jumped and caught herself on the wall to avoid giving him a reason to laugh. "Don't do that!"

"I want to speak with you first." His face was all too serious.

She tried to move around him. "Get out of my way."

"Wait," he said as he caught her arm.

"Let go of me."

"Just listen." He waited to be sure she wasn't going to argue. "You need to know what you're doing in here. Michael has a hard time controlling himself with you. We all do." He glanced down to the line of flesh visible down her V-neck.

"What?" She laughed. When she tried to move under his arm, he blocked her again.

"I'm serious, Tori. You radiate a smell like Michael's. There is something in your blood. It smells like—mimosas."

"What are you talking about?"

"Think of it like perfume. He thinks it may be why your fiancé attacked you." His shoulders drooped suddenly, as though he had deflated. "Promise me. We would never hurt you on purpose, but you shouldn't tease with more than you're willing to give."

"Okay."

Jonas' hand stroked her shoulder and his power prickled along her skin. Her body began to moisten for him and her nipples hardened as if he'd done more than simply touch her shoulder.

"I get the fucking point." She pushed past him. The last thing she needed was another vampire after her.

* * * *

Michael stood in the hallway and watched her push Jonas away. Jonas knew about the bond, which would have sent her into fits if she'd known, but he kept the secret. Even though he wanted her almost as badly as Michael did. "Is there a problem here?"

"No. Everything's just fine." She faked a smile in his direction.

"Good. Come here, love." He said the last word in a playful tone that came out wrong. It held more warning than it should have. Still, she crossed the distance between them and went on her toes to give him a quick kiss on the cheek. It wasn't believable, but she was trying.

His eyes went to the firm peaks underneath the tiny white T-shirt he'd chosen for her. It accentuated the swell of her breasts and the curves of her waist, hips, and shoulders. There were no bones or hard edges to Tori, she was all curves and softness—even though telling her that would have probably insulted her. "I see that you got my package."

"Yeah. Don't you think you could have picked up something a little less slutty?"

"Yeah, but I wouldn't have enjoyed it half as much." He motioned toward the dingy door at the end of the hall. She moved ahead of him until he pushed the door open to the outside. A limo stretched in front of them, nestled in the alleyway. The driver held the door open and she slipped inside. He nodded his thanks to the driver and moved inside behind her. The door shut quietly behind him.

He slid closer, while Tori settled into her seat. The vehicle lurched forward, but she didn't look at him at all until the vehicle sped up at an intersection. He glanced down to see her thigh exposed between the shorts and top of her boot. It looked smooth and warm. If he reached, would she jump?

Suddenly she glanced at him. "What else do I need to know about *The Scene*?"

"There are a few words that might be helpful if you knew. First, if someone asks if you're mine, say yes."

She scrunched her face.

"Want to be taken by someone else?" He waited for a few moments, and then added. "There are safe words. Usually the people there use the green light idea. Red, green, and yellow are safe words. Red means stop, of course."

"I still don't understand why they do this."

Her eyes focused on his as if she could somehow see his answer, or the truth within it, but he didn't look away. "Is man's very nature not to dominate his environment and all around him?"

Tori didn't answer.

"Dom-ing another means to take the submissive's needs as first priority. Pleasing that person is the most important thing. A man who doesn't have the stomach for that is weak."

"Some of this is abuse."

"What you call abuse, detective, is another woman's foreplay."

She laughed.

"You were aroused in my office by what many women would call harassment, were you not?"

She stared out the window.

"A dom has to focus on his submissive and it takes a great deal of time and care."

"You don't care about all the women you fuck."

"Don't presume so much, Tori." He hooked an arm around her headrest. "You might be surprised."

"Don't lie. You don't love them."

"No, I don't. But don't assume that I care nothing for them either."

"Complex emotions for a bloodsucker." She didn't look at him.

"Imagine being tied to my bed. Blindfolded. Unable to stop me from doing everything I want." His hand brushed her hair and he could hear the soft intake of air at her lips. "I know what you want, even more than you do." Michael's finger traced her shoulder as she closed her eyes. "Do you admit that the thought turns you on?"

She shrugged.

"You resist me more than any other woman I've ever known." His finger stroked her neck. "I enjoy it." He heard her heart thumping in her chest. He felt the rush of her adrenaline heating her body. The smell of her skin, of a woman's warm flesh, began to fill the limo, and it made his teeth throb.

She cut her eyes to him. "And if I didn't, you wouldn't be interested."

He laughed a full, throaty sound. "You can't fight who you truly are and neither can I. So that will never be a problem between us."

"There is no *us*." She pushed his hand off her shoulder. "I'm not playing this little slap-and-tickle game. I'll never be one of those bimbos you've got calling you master and pining over you while you sleep."

"I hope not."

"Good, 'cause we're going to find this killer and that's it. Nothing else." Tori narrowed her eyes. "Got it?"

"Of course." Michael's hand reached for her thigh and she pulled away. He placed his hand on the seat between them. "We're back to this?"

Tori nodded and let out a long sigh. They'd already gone too far. Jonas' little reminder had been exactly what she needed to remember her real place in this world. "I just can't do this with you, Michael."

"I think it's best that if, when we enter, I influence your emotions so that you feel, temporarily, as though you are my lover."

Tori laughed. "That's okay."

"Then let's deal with the unease." He reached for her again.

She jerked away.

"You have a better suggestion?"

She folded her arms across her waist. "I'm not having sex with you again."

"There is something different between us. You felt it last night."

It was just lust, a simple body-chemical reaction. One that could get her into so much trouble if he was really a suspect. "Nothing. Just lust, Michael."

"On the contrary, lust is everything, dear."

Something in his words made her heart skip a beat. She gripped her hand into a fist and tried to pain the need away. Out the window, tall buildings were giving way to smaller ones and warehouses that she watched to distract herself.

"Stop pretending. We don't have time and even your heart betrays you."

"Don't do that."

"Don't be ridiculous. I hear your heartbeat as you hear the hum of lights overhead or the wind in the trees." He leaned in and the closeness of him made her skin tingle. His head moved closer to her neck. "Now, we will only practice the simplest of touches."

"Don't you fucking bite me, Michael."

His voice came in a whisper that blew across her skin. "I won't do anything that you don't beg me to do."

She shivered. "I don't beg."

"Neither do I, *Amante*." He was still, probably listening again. He planted a soft kiss on her skin that made her heart speed up.

"I can taste your fear." His hands made a cool line up her arms to her shoulders. "I can smell how excited you are." He stroked one hand down the curve of her thigh and over the edge of her shorts. "Sooner or later, you will stop fighting."

She took a hard breath and tried to laugh, but it fell apart. "Arrogant bastard."

He pushed his hand under the hem of her shirt and felt along her ribs. Another kiss landed on her shoulder.

"We're not doing this." She grabbed his hand but didn't push. Her breath came out in short bursts that she tried to control.

He bent toward her neck, almost kissing it. Almost touching it with his lips while he pushed his hand up to cup her braless breast. "I believe we are."

She turned to face him. He pressed forward. His mouth quickly found her pulse. He sucked softly, making her heart pound in her ears. She closed her eyes when the world began to sway. She was ready and most of her was willing. But that little part wouldn't let go. "Michael."

He didn't stop. His warm hand massaged her breast and twisted the soft flesh until her nipple throbbed.

"Michael—we." Tori's body jolted from another torque and she gasped. "Not now."

He wasn't swayed by the request. His mouth moved to her ear. His breath blew across her neck as he took her earlobe in his mouth. He rolled it slowly over his tongue, then let it slide out under the pressure of his fang. The pain was small and pleasurable, making her body go loose.

"We could," he whispered. "We could do it right here. In the limo. I could bend you over this seat and take you from behind."

Her body shook with the thought.

"Or I could shove you down and get very acquainted with the inside of your thighs."

Oh. God. She turned and tried to catch his mouth in a kiss and he dodged her.

"But." He moved away slowly. "You're right. We probably shouldn't."

Tori blinked at him, then looked out the window. Rage blossomed in her chest. She wanted him now, but she would not go after him. She wouldn't lower herself to chasing him like the other women always did. No, she wasn't his plaything. And she never would be.

Chapter Seven

THE LIMO slowed in front of a large warehouse along the bay, with a three-part yin-yang type symbol painted on old brick. The only windows were high and painted black, giving the illusion that it was dark inside, but they were there. Even Tori could feel their power reaching for her in the darkness.

Michael stepped out and offered her a hand. "Leave your phone and keys here. They will be safe."

She nodded, took his hand as she stood, and then walked beside him toward the door. It opened automatically. She glanced up, along the edge of the building, then around them. No video cameras. Michael squeezed her hand and she nodded. Time to turn off the internal detective.

They stepped into a narrow corridor and followed it until they reached a staircase. They descended into darkness so thick that she took a deep breath to combat the feeling of suffocation. At the bottom, another door opened and let out a flood of heavy metal sounds.

The warehouse club buzzed with black and leather. Michael led her through the crowd of dancers. Each glanced at him, first with attitude, then nodded or gave him a small bow and moved to let them through. If she hadn't already seen the weight his name carried on the street, she'd have been impressed.

On the other side of the room, he led her into another dim room, almost identical to the other, except for the metallic stench of blood and the cold weight of several vampires trying to read her at once.

"Holy shit." She stumbled.

Michael squeezed her hand. "It's okay. They're more worried about you."

They weaved around tables and passed a line of booths. Inside each, patrons indulged their vices with minimal privacy. One girl looked up and smiled at her as another girl drank blood from her wrist in long gulps. In the next booth, two older women in Goth clothing lapped at blood that flowed from tiny holes in the full breasts of another, who had that blank stare of someone under the *affascinare*. A cold shiver went down Tori's back and she closed her eyes.

When she opened them again, a small Japanese girl sat with an overweight man at her feet who wore only a studded dog collar. He drank from a dog dish on the floor, then raised his head to growl at her, allowing blood to flow down his chin.

Tori jumped, and Michael yanked her into the next semicircle leather booth.

He smiled. "You can shut your mouth now."

"I can't. If the guys could see this, it'd—"

He nodded and put his finger to her lips. "That's enough."

Tori closed her mouth and tried not to think, but Michael grabbed a black whip that lay curled around a small glass orb that held purple rose blossoms on the table. She quirked a brow at him.

"I don't suppose you're interested?" When she just stared at him, he shrugged and ran the length of the whip through his hands. "Your loss."

* * * *

From the corner of his eye, Michael watched the bartender thumb in their direction. He was talking to Noelle, Castillo's *protégé* and head waitress. He tried to listen, but Tori drowned out their voices as she rambled on about the numerous laws being broken around them.

He reached under the table and put his hand on hers. It was supple beneath his and made him wonder if the rest of her was as warm. He felt her anxiety burn with rage, then melt away. When she glared at him, he gave her that smile again and she looked away.

Footsteps approached behind him, interrupted periodically by a woman's voice. She asked repeatedly, "Are you guys okay here?"

Good, a drink might help Tori calm down, if Noelle could keep her mouth shut.

The slim brunette appeared beside the curtain and smiled. "Evening, Michael."

"Noelle." He gave her a slight nod as she slid into the booth beside him. Tori's hand jerked from beneath his almost immediately. *Dammit.*

"Castillo said to make you welcome this evening." She slipped a black nail across the mound of breast that peeked out over the tight black dress. A bit of blood pooled on the surface. She smiled and moved closer so that a wave of hunger rolled over him. "And to give you anything you want."

He felt Tori's jealousy hit him like pinpricks across his face and he glanced at her. Her eyes narrowed slightly. She wouldn't understand this. She'd hold it against him, but refusing would insult both Noelle and Castillo. A little jealousy was worth keeping them from punishment under the *padrone's* hand. He turned back to Noelle, leaned down and made a long, quick lick over the wound. The blood was luke-warm, weak, and tasted of Castillo.

He took the girl's hand and used her nail to cut a bit of his wrist. She gave him a little pout, but took the blood with all the enthusiasm she probably expected him to have for the breast wound. Her lips locked tight over his flesh and sucked a little too hard. He felt the force of her pull. His cock twitched.

Tori huffed and the sound drew his attention.

The girl released him with a slurp and wiped her mouth with her fingertips. As she leaned back, a cattish grin spread her lips. "Welcome, Michael. All that is Castillo's is yours."

"Thank you, Noelle."

She moved her attention to Tori. "Can I get you any-thing?"

Tori's face took an angry twist. Somehow, he couldn't feel what she was thinking, and she didn't speak. "Noelle, I think she'll have a glass of Pinot Grigio."

"Don't order for me. Noelle, I want a Jack and Coke."

"Alright." The woman slipped from the booth and gave them a slight bow. She walked away, rolling her hips in a slow, seductive pace.

He turned his attention back toward Tori. "A *shiava* does not speak to her *Dominatore* that way."

"I'm not your—"

Don't. He threw the thought at her and she stopped. "We are in my realm and you will do as I say." She opened her mouth to argue, but he glared at her and continued. "Under-stood, Detective?"

She nodded, still angry. *Fuck you*, she thought.

"Don't let your jealousy get the best of you, *Amante*."

She laughed. "You think I'm—"

"Lying is a waste of time."

She turned her face toward the bar and crossed her arms. From the side, he could see how long her lashes were. They were long enough to threaten her brows, but the effect was so subtle that they didn't look fake. She was beautiful and when she huffed, forcing her breasts up and down, he remembered how she had looked in his dream with her hands bound in the lamplight.

He leaned forward. "Look at me."

She didn't budge.

"I said look at me, Victoria."

She turned her head slowly toward him.

He took her face in his hands, leaned forward, and placed his lips against hers softly. It was a slow kiss that let him feel the fullness of her bottom lip. Her lipstick tasted of warm cherries. She closed her eyes, and he felt her tension drain slowly away with a sigh that parted her lips.

He let a low growl roll from his mouth, and pushed his tongue inside with a teasing stroke. But, when she pressed forward, he pulled away.

She blinked her eyes open. "What?"

"That's enough for now."

Victoria looked thoroughly confused. Good, she needed to feel confusion. She'd been in control for too long, and not because she preferred to be. He'd bet that she'd never been with a man who truly knew how to bed a woman. Most of these modern pussies who called themselves men didn't have a clue what they were doing. They left all the responsibility to their women. Pathetic.

Noelle appeared again, winked in his direction. She slid the drink on the table and left without a word.

"Thank you, Noelle."

Tori glanced from the woman to him and back. "She's pretty hot for you."

He shrugged.

Jonas appeared, dressed in his bondage best--latex pants and an open black wife-beater shirt, the type of thing he wore only to perform or snag female attention. He slipped into the booth on the other side of Tori and smiled at her a little too brightly.

"Nice of you to join us," Michael said.

He nodded to him, then looked back at Tori. "Like the club?"

Tori snarled her lip and shook her head. When Jonas feigned shock, she took a long drink and let her eyes roam the room. All she needed was Damon. When he was locked away, or dead, this would all be over, and she could go back to normal life.

Jonas put his arm on the back of the booth and twisted his body toward her. "You don't like the idea of doing exactly what you want and having no one around to judge you for it?"

"Someone's always judging you, Jonas."

Michael swallowed hard enough that even she heard it and glanced around.

"No, they're not." He leaned a little closer and it drew her attention. The smell of his cologne made her nose twitch. "If I took you right here, no one would care."

Michael cleared his throat. "Don't be so sure."

She looked at him, and he looked back, but nothing in those eyes indicated how he really felt.

Jonas' hand went to her shoulder and drew her attention back to him. "Trust me, if I fucked you on top of this table, the most we'd get is applause."

"That's enough, Jonas."

Jonas let a flash of defiance show on his face, and then glanced around the room as if he wasn't talking to Michael. "Any news?"

"Nothing. We haven't been here long."

"Well, here comes trouble."

Tori glanced down the side where Jonas was looking, but couldn't quite see around the privacy wall. She breathed in slowly, trying to make her heart stop the slow progression it made toward a fast heart rate, and waited.

Damon came into view, followed closely by a girl who couldn't have been more than sixteen or seventeen, with bottle black hair, a tartan plaid miniskirt, and black crop top. She didn't look up at them when he stopped at the end of the table, but Tori could still see that her black mascara and eyeliner were dribbling down her cheeks.

The man smirked. "What brings you here?"

"I came to visit my *padrone*." Michael gripped her hand under the table.

"Why?"

Jonas leaned forward, obviously trying to take control of the conversation. "We—"

"I don't owe you an explanation."

"If you want to see Castillo, you do," Damon said.

"Then, you have my explanation."

"Why do you want to see him?"

Michael sat a little straighter. "Damon, you're starting to annoy me. My *shiava* and I just wanted to enjoy the club and say hello to Castillo."

"You mean the cop?" Damon motioned toward her with his chin.

Tori's heart jumped. How did he know? Well, it was possible that he could have found out from anyone, but it was still unnerving to have him just throw it out there like that.

"That is her human job, but she is mine—first and foremost." Michael smiled in her direction.

"She is still a cop."

"Yes."

"You bloody fool." He leaned forward, palms on the table, eyeing Tori and sending a whiff of alcohol their way. "I didn't know who you were when we last met, or I would have taken you. If Michael doesn't take you soon, Castillo tells me that I may have his permission to do the deed."

Jonas looked down, shook his head, and smiled. The testosterone was starting to run a little too deep.

Michael batted one of his hands off the table and almost sent him over. "Fuck you, Damon."

"Do something—anything." The man leaned back and waved his hands wide, almost smacking the girl in the head, but she didn't flinch. "This is our place. You have no authority here."

A chuckle came from Michael. "When you push me too far, it won't matter if your daddy's around. You're just his newest toy."

Damon's hands gripped into fists so tight that his knuckles went white. "You will have that day…soon."

"Yes, I will."

The man stood, staring at Michael for a long moment. When he moved, it was to give a slight bow to Jonas, then to Tori. As he turned to walk away, he smirked. "Enjoy the club."

Tori arched a brow at Michael, who smiled halfheartedly.

Jonas leaned forward, resting his elbows on the table. "Well, this should get interesting now."

"Be ready." Michael gave Tori a quick pat on the leg. "I don't know what they'll do."

"Great. So I should worry?"

Jonas winked in her direction. "That probably wouldn't be a bad idea."

"Just remember what we discussed."

She nodded. That was easy enough, depending on what exactly they were about to get into. She knew it would be tough, but hadn't expected Michael to pick a fight with him right off the bat.

"Excuse me." Noelle appeared in front of the table. "My master invites you to enjoy a private chamber. If you'll follow me, I will show you to it."

"Thank you." Michael slipped from the booth and held his hand out to Tori. "Please tell your master that it is much appreciated."

Tori glared at him and hoped he could feel her anger, but took his hand. After he helped her up, she jerked her hand away. Coming into the club after a killer was one thing. Going into a spank and tickle room with vampires was something else.

They followed the girl to a black leather-padded door that stood between the bathrooms and displayed a silver sign that read *VIPs Only*. Inside was a long corridor with red lighting that ended at a hall that went right and left. They turned left and stopped at the third door, number twenty-seven.

Noelle turned the knob and pushed the door open. Her arm made a sweeping gesture toward the opening. "Enjoy."

Jonas was the first to enter and Tori followed.

* * * *

"Thank you," Michael said and walked inside the black room. It was almost identical to the other rooms at *The Scene*, with dark furniture, mirrors, various bondage tools, a display of whips and floggers, and a tub for those who were into water bondage.

Tori stood there with a hand over her mouth. Her eyes focused on the far wall. He followed her gaze to a woman chained to the wall with her arms above her head. Her body was stripped down to a black thong and black boots, her blonde hair hung loosely above perfectly rounded hips, and a deep purple blindfold was knotted behind her head.

The door shut behind them with a muffled thud, leaving them with the baited trap. Castillo knew he was bringing the detective and her reputation. She would never go for it. But if they didn't play along, they'd be punished legally, under the *Alleanza*.

* * * *

Tori tried not to be angry. There was no way Michael could have known about the woman, unless he'd arranged it with Castillo. If he had, then perhaps it could make their plan even more convincing. If he hadn't, then Castillo was testing their bond. Either way, leaving meant risking everything, including her job and their lives.

She glanced at Michael. When she opened her mouth, his finger covered her lips. He slipped an arm around her and she let him pull her close. Even that wonderful smell of him couldn't stop her from feeling a bit queasy at the thought of what was to come.

"Don't say anything too loud." When his mouth loomed close to her ear, she could feel that warm breath on her skin, and she closed her eyes to keep her mind from wandering toward the way that his mouth almost brushed her earlobe. "She is human and may hear."

Tori nodded as he continued. "She is an offering. We may refuse, but without good reason, the *padrone* may choose to enforce the old laws. So, we must bed her as Castillo intends, and feed from her."

She was not going to stand here and watch Michael have sex with someone else. Not that he was hers, or that they were in a relationship. It was just the creep-out factor.

She whispered back to him. "I can't watch."

"Castillo's simply looking for a reason to kill you and end this. He cannot under *The Alleanza*."

Tori opened her eyes and cut them toward him. Michael was so close that she only saw the shoulder of his suit jacket. "Why?"

"You are under my protection."

Something about it made her feel warm inside. She fought back a smile as she rolled her eyes up to look at Jonas, who stood watching the woman sway in her chains, like a cat watching a butterfly on a daisy. "You don't expect me to be a part—"

"Just do as I ask and everything will be fine."

She wished she could read his mind. Didn't he know that this was way past being polite? They were in pretty-fucking-weird territory.

Michael brushed her cheek with his hand. "Trust me."

She let out a long breath. "Alright."

He motioned Jonas close, and whispered something in his ear. The man nodded, then moved toward the woman.

Michael turned Tori so that her back was against his chest. His arms stroked up and down her arms while she watched Jonas unhook the girl. When he turned her, there were fading bruises on her full breasts, which were obviously fake, because as he led her to the center of the room by the short chain between her cuffs, the fleshy mounds refused to move with the sway of her hips.

Tori glanced up at Jonas' face to see a menacing grin turn up the corners of his lips. He hooked the handcuffs to a pole in front of the girl, then moved around behind her. He slapped her hard on the ass. "Spread 'em."

Tori's heart leapt as the woman moved her feet shoulder-length apart. Her head bowed slightly, as though she await-ed his next command, while Jonas slipped off his shirt and tossed it onto the couch. Tori had seen him shirtless before, but in the dim light, his abs looked enticingly well-defined.

He moved behind the woman, centered himself, and stroked his hands slowly up her hips. He followed the curves of her body, but his eyes watched Tori. The woman let out a shaky sigh.

"Will you obey your master?" Jonas spoke in a sultry tone as his hand smoothed the crescent line under the woman's breasts. Lust crept into those eyes and the room filled with a low buzz that made everything seem to vibrate.

Tori's nipples hardened and Michael went still behind her.

"Yes." The woman moaned as he twisted one of her nipples.

Jonas' emotion increased, making the room's vibration turn into a loud ripple that flooded past Tori's boundaries. She clenched her fist, trying to avoid the erotic trip that Jonas seemed set on dragging her on.

Michael took her hands in his and wrapped his arms around her, folding their hands in front of her waist. He pulled her back so that the curves of their bodies met, then whispered against her neck. "Let it happen this time. It must be believable. Trust me. I will protect you."

The sensation flushed her face and made her skin alight with need. She could feel the pulse between her legs, throbbing for touch.

"You see, Jonas can read her mind. He has that gift and knows everything she wants."

Michael's breath against her neck made her tremble. She put her full weight against his chest so that she could feel him hard against her. She tried to let herself ease into the vampire's trick.

Jonas' hands snaked down the front of the woman's panties, then dipped in a slow tease. The other hand smoothed around the mound of her breast. The woman rocked her hips against his hand, riding his fingers.

Suddenly Jonas unhooked the girl, turned her quickly, and then secured her again to the pole with her hands over her head and her back against it. With her lithe body stretched in front of them, it was obvious that her nipples were swollen and red.

Jonas bent so that Tori and Michael could see, and took one in his teeth. Tori felt the pain in her own skin, then felt the pull as he slowly dragged way. It was the same trick he used in the show. It had been so long since she'd let it happen that she'd forgotten how real it felt.

He moved to the other side and repeated the tease, sending every sensation toward Tori so that she ached.

"Oh, Master." The girl shivered. "Let me please you."

"You'll get your chance." He stood straight and pulled the girl's head to one side. He motioned Tori toward them.

She took a step toward him, but Michael yanked her back. She frowned up at him.

"I won't let you do something you'll regret," Michael whispered.

Jonas grumbled something she couldn't hear. When she looked, he crooked a finger.

Michael said, "I said no, Jonas."

Jonas kept his eyes locked on Tori as he slipped his hand inside the woman's panties again. His hand stroked her in slow motion.

When the girl moaned, Tori trembled and took a deep breath. That lust came over her in waves. It pushed at the soft flesh between her legs and she felt the ghost hand of his power pushing at her, bringing her toward the brink. She wanted to swap places with the slave, to take his pleasure, even if it was just the *trucchi* and not real passion.

Michael's lips brushed her shoulder.

Sparks of heat danced up to her face. She gasped and felt his grip tighten around her. Her eyes shut when he kissed a line up her neck. He lingered near her pulse and it made her heart race. If they were alone, she'd turn and give him what he wanted. But they weren't alone and anything she did here would spread like wildfire through the vampire community. Besides, there were probably cameras.

The girl gasped loudly and Tori opened her eyes. Jonas was now in front of her. He held her round hips while he thrust inside her. Each of his moves sent electric waves through the room. Tori throbbed. She wanted him. All of him. Right now.

With one exhale, Tori fell into the act. She closed her eyes again and arched her neck up to him. When she spoke, her voice sounded soft and sleepy. "Let's leave."

He let out a growling sound that made her stomach clench. Michael's lips clamped on her neck. His hands held her stomach and pushed her against his erection.

Jonas made a guttural sound that forced Tori's eyes open. She watched him rip the girl's handcuffs apart, pin her to the pole, and bury his face in her neck. A breeze flew through the room, whipping Tori's hair.

All that lust suddenly turned to a brilliant white satisfaction that felt almost like afterglow. She could taste the warm copper on Jonas' tongue. Tori knew he'd bitten her, but she couldn't stop watching. Instead, she bit her lip and let the feel of Michael nibbling at her neck bring her to the brink.

Michael suddenly stopped and pulled her around to face him. "Come on."

Chapter Eight

TORI STEPPED out into the private underground hallway at Michael's club. If it hadn't been for Jonas catching them, then riding with them in the limo, she'd have been naked by now.

Something primal in her responded to Michael like it did to no one else, and she couldn't keep pushing it back. Vampire or not. She couldn't have a real relationship with him, but it could be just sex. It didn't have to be messy.

She followed him ahead. The sound of their footsteps echoed off the walls. Either no one was down here, or the rooms were soundproof.

When Michael stopped to swipe the key in the card slot beside the steel door, it was too quiet. There was a beep, and he turned the knob to open the door and cast a beam of light into the dark chamber, illuminating an ornate four-poster bed. He flicked a switch and dim lights filled the room with a yellowish glow, just as the door shut again. It was a strange deviation from Michael's other rooms, simply because it was so ordinary. It looked just like any room in any other old home, filled with antiques, tapestries, old weapons, and candles.

Tori turned to see him watching her closely. Her hand reached to place her cell phone and keys on the dresser beside the door, but her eyes stayed on him. "What?"

He closed the distance between them and brought that wonderful scent of his to her nostrils. "Please stop shutting me out, Victoria."

"I'm not."

"Then relax." His hands smoothed hair away from her face.

She closed her eyes and focused on how his hands were rough against her skin. They were warm and moved along her face, gliding down her neck, over her shoulders, and finally her arms.

Michael's scent brought the feel of him, as if it were a tangible thing that rubbed her cheek and whispered across her skin. She breathed it in deeply and felt his hunger for her body and for her blood. Raw need. And loneliness. The man and the monstrous thing inside him were in agreement. They would have her soon.

He caught her again in a hungry kiss that melted away the rest of her resistance like wax in a flame. He pulled them together, bowing Tori's body against his so that she felt how solid he was, the way he felt in her dreams. For that moment, the world was all him. His mouth, his shoulders, and his hands sliding over her.

Her head swam when he lifted her off the floor. She struggled to breathe and pulled back just as he sat her on the bed. She reached for his shirt, caught it, and popped the buttons off so hard that a few pinged on the stone floor. Her fingers smoothed over taut skin, up the ridges of muscle, and then smoothed the shirt down his arms.

His mouth moved to her neck and his arms pushed hers away. Michael's fingers looped over the neck of her shirt and ripped it right down the center. His eyes went to her chest and his hands smoothed the skin there, gently cupping her breasts as if they were glass.

She fumbled at his pants and finally managed to open them. With a shove, they fell to the floor, but Tori didn't get to touch him. Instead, he shoved her back onto the bed and went to work on her black shorts.

In a flash, he worked them down over her boots. They flew backwards over his shoulder, along with her panties. Then his hands slid up the front of her thighs. His eyes were dark and surges of his power filled the room until she gasped for air as he followed the lines to where her legs and hips connected.

She looked down the line of her belly and saw his pale abdomen with its line of dark hair that ended at an amazing shaft. He glanced up at her, then back to his hand, pressing his palm over her center. She watched him stroke up and down, then dip a finger inside.

She closed her eyes and rolled her hips to him, but heard him let out a low growl and felt his free hand push her hip back to the bed. She was swollen, wet, and all but begging him, but he wouldn't be rushed.

Michael pulled his hands away. He lowered his body to hers and took her mouth again.

Her nipples ached, urged on by the weight of his chest while his hips prepared to penetrate her. She opened her eyes, then leaned forward to take his lower lip between her teeth.

He moaned, grabbed her wrists, and pulled them over her head. His weight trapping her added to the delicious feel of him bending his head to her nipple. She pushed her hips toward his, trying to push him inside.

Michael pulled back. "Not yet."

"Please." She struggled to loosen her wrists, but he held her tight. His free hand twisted her nipple. The pain mixed with pleasure jolted through her body and made her insides twist. "Please, Michael."

"Don't make me tie you."

She closed her eyes. The thought made her body feel like it was vibrating. She'd always wanted it, but it was a huge risk, especially with a vampire. If anyone found out, the guys at the department would never let her forget it. And if it went really bad, she probably wouldn't be strong enough to free herself.

Michael felt her slipping toward guilt and torqued her nipple again to bring her back. She squinted her eyes and he could almost feel her trying to think of something else. "Don't think, Victoria."

"I can't do this." Her voice trembled. "Let me go."

"You don't have a choice."

He bent his head to roll her nipple between his teeth again, and she let out a long groan that gave him chills. Then came the thought of tying her again, but this time he didn't put it there. She wanted it. No, she needed him to because she would never do it on her own.

"Let me go." Her voice held a hint of mock fear.

"Alright, I warned you."

He manipulated his legs over hers to pin her down, then used his free hand to reach down between the mattress and headboard. He'd been hoping for this since the first time he saw her watching the show. She wanted to be bound, to be taken, but she couldn't bring herself to say it.

"What are you doing?" Her voice edged real concern.

His cock twitched, adding to the ache he already felt. The dark part of him loved her fear and how it tasted like sour candies on his tongue. He pulled the length of silken rope, then quickly wrapped her wrists and tied them over her head so that she wasn't stretched too tight, but couldn't lower her arms, either.

He leaned back and smiled down at her.

She struggled against the ropes, making her beautiful tits jiggle. "Let me go."

"Don't make me gag you, too."

Tori stopped talking and glared at him, but the room filled with the sweet scent of her excitement, and it made him throb.

Michael moved back down, spreading her legs with his knees as she closed her eyes. A wave of anxiety rolled through the room. She was scared and excited. The devil inside him stirred and begged for her neck, wanted to drain her dry, while what was left of the human that he had been pushed him back. He had to get control or he would ruin the entire experience for her. He swallowed hard and tried not to feel her need.

"You're going to do exactly what I say. What happens in this room will never again be discussed. Ever. With anyone." He reached into the nightstand and grabbed a black satin sleep mask. She did little more than stare at him curiously, as he tucked it over her head. He waved his hand close to her face to make sure she couldn't see. "You are here for my pleasure and anything you do to the contrary will be punished. Do you understand?"

She nodded. Good. She was getting into the role.

* * * *

Tori took a deep breath. She would not let her conservative self take over again. She wanted this. Hell, she'd wanted this since the first day she met him. Something inside her craved it, and if he truly wouldn't tell, then she was a fool not to let it happen.

"Don't speak until I say that you can." His hands gripped her thighs, then smoothed up her naked hips.

She imagined what she must look like laid out on the bed while Michael crouched between her legs that were clad only in black knee boots. She couldn't fight the smile that came with a little twinge of embarrassment. She wanted him to take her, but the vulnerability made her question the decision. She was laid bare on his bed, with him holding her most private areas open for full view.

"You are never to hide this body from me again." His hands smoothed over her hips and traced down to her clean-shaven lips. The sensation made her back arch. Suddenly she was glad she'd made the effort to do the extra shaving.

Michael's fingers pushed between the folds and pulled her open. He stroked her erect clit, drawing out long moans. When he slipped a finger inside her, she didn't hold back a loud gasp. She wasn't going to last long.

"You are going to come before I fuck you. But only when I tell you to."

His finger slid out, then back in, joined with another in a slow, wet stroke. His thumb worked circles around her button, which made her thighs shake. Inside, the fingers parted then went together again.

Her body jolted.

Michael let out a low groan and the ripples of his power began to flow over her faster. His fingers curved upward and stroked her insides until they found the spot. Tori arched her back again, pushing her rear against the bed as the first spasm spread from her toes upward. She was about to pop and he still hadn't said she could. It was a fun game, but she was about to break his rules. "Michael. *Please.*"

"I told you." He slipped his fingers out. "There is no talking."

She could feel him moving off the bed. She fought to see from a tiny corner of light under the mask and struggled against the ropes. "Where are you going?"

She heard his feet padding across the stone floor. She struggled harder, yanking at the ropes. "Michael?"

He was going to leave her tied. *Dammit.* "Don't you leave me here!"

"The more you do that, the longer I'll be gone."

The door opened and shut.

She yelled out her frustration. This wasn't a game anymore. "You bastard!"

* * * *

Michael watched from his position beside the door as Tori kicked the bed one last time. Her arms had to hurt from struggling this long. He wanted to walk over, give her a soft kiss, warm her flesh, and ease her struggle, but it'd be worth it in the end. She had to embrace her real desires or she'd be running from them forever.

She bit her lip and the anger cooled into sadness.

"Are you ready to behave?"

Her head jerked in the direction of his voice. She was still for a moment, flexing her jaw, before she finally nodded her head.

He smiled to himself and pushed away from the wall. "Be good or I'll really leave. Understood?"

She nodded as he climbed back on the bed, between her legs. He pushed them open gently, and her knees began to shake. He knew what it was like to submit to someone else for the first time, to release control, and he didn't need to feel her fear envelop him to know that she was scared. Still, the mixture of her fear and desire was intoxicating.

* * * *

Tori wanted to slap him, and then kiss him, but when Michael's fingers went to work between her legs again, the first thought faded.

His mouth caressed her inner thigh. It lingered and edged toward her, bringing back the pleasure of her bondage. His tongue slipped a circle around her clit and then his lips sucked it inside. Her hips convulsed against him and he laughed wickedly. Michael stroked that spot again, as his mouth worked with the skill that only centuries of practice could bring.

Her flesh burned and she could feel that familiar tension working its way up her spine. She was almost there, and if he stopped her this time, she'd shoot him.

Tori groaned as he said, "You can come now."

The fingers spread again, then made a circle over her spot as his teeth brushed her tiny button. When he gently bit her clit, the climax exploded through her. He didn't stop. Instead, he continued to stroke and nibble until the frenzy left her breathless and dazed.

As he pulled away, she lay wasted, unable to move or even care that he was probably staring at her. A pleased glow warmed her body while the aftershocks faded. She hadn't been this satisfied for years, if ever, and the foolish grin on her face probably told him so.

She felt the warm stiffness of Michael's erection tease her slit. It slid up and down, snaking over her sensitive clit so that she jerked with each stroke. The sensation was too loud, too sharp, and she fought to pull back.

Slowly, he worked her into another frenzy of hunger that made her hips tilt toward him and her back arch. Then he moved, grabbed her side, and rolled her onto her stomach.

Tori pulled herself onto her elbows just as he spread her legs. He centered himself and found her opening with his tip just before he grabbed her hips. She was wet enough that he buried himself inside her in one hard thrust that stretched her skin tight. He was deep in her belly, pushing against the walls, but there was no pain like there had been with Robert. Maybe he'd never taken enough time to please her.

Each time Michael pulled out and then pushed back inside, Tori's body tightened harder than she'd ever imagined possible. She quaked again, and another orgasm erupted inside, pinging around in her core until she let it flow with a long yell.

Michael made one final thrust. He stiffened against her and plunged as deeply as he could go. His fingers dug into her hips and his fluids spilled into her.

* * * *

"Untie me." Tori panted, still blindfolded.

Michael was on the bed beside her with his legs wrapped around hers. His hand played slowly through her hair and she was sure he was staring at her. "I think I'm going to keep you right here, just like this."

He pulled the mask off her in a quick move that left her blinking against the dim light. Somehow, being able to see made her more aware of her nudity. She laughed, half-afraid that he was serious. "And who would catch the killer?"

"I'll take care of him." He smiled down at her, propped on one elbow. "I've been waiting to drink that bastard dry."

"The Chief would send a S.W.A.T. team in here after me and the whole *Alleanza* would be blown."

He smirked. "They wouldn't make it through the front door, *inamorato*." He traced a finger down her spine and over the curve of her ass. "Face it, you're mine now."

"Don't get possessive." She wanted to ask what *inamorato* meant, but his possessiveness was more important.

He slapped her hard on the rear, and the sting made her cringe. "Do I need to punish you again?"

"No." She shook her head and tried not to grin. "I think I've had all the punishment I can handle for one night."

"I thought so."

His reached over her head and untied her. He rubbed her wrists, then kissed each one gently. It was the gentlest of touches, followed by his arm wrapping around her.

It was too gentle. Michael looked at her with such adoration. She'd even venture to call it love. It couldn't be that. No vampire let anyone, especially a human, get this close. He was up to something. He had to be. "What time is it? I need to go home."

He pulled her to him, snuggling her into the hollow of his side. "You're staying here with me tonight."

"I have to go to work."

"You are working, remember?" He grabbed a remote off the nightstand, flicked the lights off, and then settled back.

Her heart ached suddenly. Was that what he thought of her surrender that evening? Work? Maybe she was taking this far too seriously. The point was to have a nice bit of sex with him, get the killer, and walk away. She just had to stay focused.

He kissed her on the forehead and snuggled closer. "Sleep well. Tomorrow we'll work out how to get rid of Damon."

* * * *

Voices, that's what Tori was hearing. She blinked her eyes open in the dark. Beside her, Michael had grown cool, his breathing slowed to an almost inaudible level. When she moved his arm from around her, he moved. He wasn't quite dead, but almost. Another one of life's mysteries solved.

The ring of a phone erupted in the darkness and a light danced on the ceiling beside the door. Her cell. She jumped off the bed and almost tripped on her own heels. She'd forgotten to take off the boots, but didn't have time to as she darted to the phone.

She grabbed it and flipped it open. She whispered, "Hello?"

There was a grunt at the other end. "About time. Where are you?"

"Sleeping." She glanced toward the bed but couldn't really see Michael in the dark. "Who is this?"

"Joe Phillips. We've got another body. A man named Sam. I wouldn't call you on this one, but everything's the same as the other victims. Looks like the same guy. Even the bite marks. The Chief's been hunting you and I told him I'd run you down."

"Thanks."

"There's something else. I have an informant that has information on the case, but he will only talk to you. Says you'll understand why."

She scratched her head. "Okay. I'll get with him later."

"No. He says it has to be now. He wants you to meet us in twenty minutes outside the Quick-Stop on the corner of Shiloh and Third."

She let out a long yawn into the phone. She didn't want to leave Michael without word of where she was going, but she couldn't turn away possibly good information. "Alright. I'll be there."

Chapter Nine

TORI PULLED up in front of the Quick-Stop and threw the shifter into Park. There were a few cars along the other side of the building, but it was deserted on her side near the alley. The sun was setting and most of the city already lay covered in a blanket of shadow. She took a long drink of her soda. It wasn't cappuccino, but it helped to wake her up.

Officer Joe, in his starched uniform, peered around the corner and waved her over. She grabbed the phone, tucking it in her pocket as she opened the car door. Thankfully, her apartment wasn't far, so she'd had time to change into jeans and a black tee. Along with it, she added the badge that hung from her belt.

She closed the door behind her and walked to the edge of the building. "Evening, Joe."

"Sorry I had to wake you. Putting in late hours?"

"Always."

"Where's your friend?"

"He's back here." He motioned further into shadows.

Something felt wrong as she looked down the corridor. Her skin tingled and her nerves seemed to jump into overdrive. She checked the gun tucked into the back of her pants and walked beside Joe to keep an eye on him. "What's his name?"

"Good evening, Detective."

The voice carried a distinct accent, though she couldn't tell what kind. She squinted harder and saw the man emerge from the shadows. Not really emerge as much as separate himself from them, as if he were part of the shadow itself.

The hair on the back of her neck stood up and she folded her hands behind her back, hoping to look casual and stay close to the gun. "Evening."

His features came into view. He was about her height, with tanned skin and dark hair. His featured reminded her of all the Spanish actors she'd ever seen, exotic and sculpted. "I hope my request didn't pull you away from anything *important*. I know that you were out quite late last evening."

How could he—It was him. "Castillo?"

"The one and only." He gave her a flourishing bow, the kind Euro-trash vamps in movies did.

She glanced at Joe, who smiled proudly, then back at the informant. "What do you want?"

"I only wish to talk. I understand that you seek my companion, Damon, because of his...." He motioned with one hand as though he were pulling the word from the air, "... hobby."

"Hobby?" She laughed. "Are you kidding me? He's a psycho."

"That is a relative term, dear."

She shook her head. The man was crazier than Michael made him out to be. "What about it?"

"I didn't realize that I had allowed his activities to venture so far outside our laws. If you had come to me, I would have surrendered him to you."

"Really? Why is that?"

"I am a slave to our laws – and our laws insist that I must abide by yours."

"Just like that?"

"Just like that."

"I don't believe you."

"I assumed you might not. So, consider this."

He was suddenly in her face. She didn't even blink. He was just there and it made her take a step back. "Don't get too close."

"I apologize." Castillo smiled and took a step back. "I am a just leader, Detective. Officer Phillips and several of your fellow city workers trust me. Even your mayor is a trusted friend."

"That's not impressing me."

"Then consider that I have allowed Michael to keep you even though he never asked my permission to begin the *vincolo* with you. You are an illegal *shiava* and I could kill both of you if I choose."

She laughed again. "See, that's where you're wrong. I have not started the *vincolo* with him."

"Yes, you have." He sniffed the air in her direction. "I smell him on you."

"There's a reason for—"

"I am not speaking of sex. His scent is in your blood. His blood is in you. There is no mistake."

Her heart thudded in her chest. She hadn't tasted his blood, not really. Not enough to create a bond. It was crazy. He was trying to bluff her.

"I sense your doubt, but I assure you that it is true. I am told that he saved your life with the *vincolo*, when your fiancé attempted to kill you. Did you not wonder how you survived such a bite?"

She shrugged. "Not really."

"Detective, do you expect me to believe that?"

"I'm not asking you to believe anything. I don't care what you think."

He nodded. "I understand your hesitation, but know that I will deal with Damon. He is no longer under my protection. You have my word."

She nodded.

He reached forward, took her hand, and lifted it to his lips. He placed an icy kiss on her skin that lingered even after he turned and walked away.

Tori waited until she no longer heard his footsteps in the alley, then turned on her heels and headed toward the car. A *vincolo*. That explained the sensations. Why she couldn't resist him. It made perfect damned sense. How could he do this to her?! They couldn't stop this without one of them dying. Better yet, how could she have been so naive?

"Tyler, you okay?"

She stopped and glanced back at Officer Joe. "Why did you do this?"

"What?"

"Why did you lure me here?"

"I—uh—I didn't mean it like that. He seemed to want to help."

She glared at him and his stupid stiff shirt. He was everything that was wrong with people who hadn't spent enough time in real life. People like her who stayed hopeful. She hung her head and walked toward the car. "Leave me alone, Joe."

* * * *

Tori stomped toward the door of *The Fallen*. The more she thought about it, the more the whole thing started to make sense. There was no way she could have survived having a hunk bitten out of her neck without *trucchi*, even if they'd used their own blood to heal it. And there was something else.

Ever since she'd met him, Michael had been in her dreams. Sometimes he seemed very, very real. Others, it seemed like a normal dream. In a very real one, he was holding her. She was naked and wanted to go to sleep, but he kept talking to her. Telling her that if she'd hold on, just a few minutes more, she'd be fine.

That had to be a memory. He'd saved her, then hid the truth.

Blane opened his mouth at the door and Tori threw up a hand. He raised a brow and opened the door for her.

She breezed past the weapons-Nazi and cruised toward the private bar. She'd find out. She'd know if Michael did it as soon as she asked him. She had to.

"Tori?"

Jonas' voice came from the bar as she passed, but she didn't slow. Instead, she moved into the private area and headed for the hallway.

Jonas must have caught up as she entered the hall because his footsteps rushed up behind her. "Tori. What's wrong?"

He grabbed her arm and she jerked it away. "Don't touch me!"

"Geez. Who peed in your Wheaties?"

She glared at him. "Where's Michael?"

"Still asleep. He can't rise as early as us. He'll be down for another hour or two. Why?"

She leaned closer to him. "Did you know he bonded us?"

He went still, completely motionless, except that he blinked at her.

"You did!" She threw up her hands and started to pace. "Dammit. How could I have been soooo—"

"Wait. Don't assume you—"

"Are you saying he didn't bond me?"

"Well…."

"That's what I thought. He's been lying to me this whole—" She screamed and stomped her foot. "I can't believe I fell for it." She whirled on him. "When he wakes up, you tell that bastard not to come near me. I knew I was right about him."

"Tori, you really need to talk to him."

"No—I—do—not."

"Wait. Who told you?"

"Don't worry about it."

"If this has something to do with Castillo—"

"Like I said, don't worry about it." She shoved past him and headed back outside.

She had to get outside for some fresh air. If she stayed in that godforsaken vampire club, she'd explode from sheer rage. She weaved quickly enough through the crowds and back out the door that no one tried to stop her.

Part of her wanted to go back and confront Michael. Another part wanted him to deny it and make her believe it wasn't true. The rest wanted to stake him and bury him in a deep hole. The last thought brought a twinge of guilt. As she pushed past a couple of Goth kids on the sidewalk, she sucked in a breath that brought tears.

She tried to blink them away, but more came. She put her head down and tried to keep her shoulders from drooping. Then, she wiped the corners of her eyes and sped up. A few more feet and she'd be in the car.

* * * *

Tori opened the door to her room and started stripping off clothes. She needed a bath. A long, hot, sanitizing one. That sickening, luscious smell of Michael needed to go. *Now*.

She put her gun on the dresser, then tossed her pants on the bed. If he'd lied to her about the bond, he was probably using her, too. That's what they always did, use humans for what they wanted. She stripped off the panties and bra, tossed them on the floor, then stepped into the bathroom.

The little gray mouse toy that Blade usually batted around sat in the middle of the floor, smiling at her.

With a quick kick, the mouse spun across the floor into the pile of dirty clothes under the sink. She turned, grabbed the edge of the blue shower curtain, and yanked it aside. Her jaw muscle flexed back and forth, even as she twisted the knob to start the warm water showering down over her head.

She looked at the lavender-vanilla bath wash she received for her birthday. The label said it was for "relaxation", but she had never tried it. Tori popped the lid, squirted a bit on the spongy body scrubber, and started to rub.

She scrubbed harder and the skin reddened. Occasionally, she stopped, sniffed her skin, then scrubbed some more.

Her wet hair matted around her face, mixing water with the tears that began to leak out. Maybe she did owe him her life, but he didn't have to lie about it. No one wanted to be forced into a relationship, especially one that made her feel stronger emotions than she would normally. She might have agreed, and she might have appreciated it if he'd explained it to her before, but it was too late now. Years too freakin' late.

She tossed the scrubber into the tub and covered her face. Tears came hard and her body rocked with the flow. It turned into a sob that even made Blade peek his head in behind the curtain. First Robert cheated, then tried to kill her, and now she was bound to one of the *vampiro* for the rest of one of their lives.

She raised her head, letting the water flow over her cheeks, then backed out of the flow. Her muscles ached and her knees felt weak. She was tired—emotionally and physically—and there was still a killer on the loose, assuming Castillo hadn't actually done anything to him. What had she been thinking? No one in their right mind would snuggle up to a man who could drain you dry in a matter of minutes and then destroy most traces of your existence.

A turn of the tap stopped the water and she stepped out onto the soft cream rug. She grabbed a towel, wrapped it around her, and headed into the bedroom. It was only seven o'clock, according to the small green digits on the clock. Maybe getting a few more hours of rest would calm her nerves.

* * * *

Michael felt the pressure of something hollow in his chest. He had the strangest urge to cry, like someone had just died. He rolled over, toward Tori.

She was gone.

"Victoria?"

There was no answer, only the faint sound of someone in the hallway outside the room. He swung his legs over the side of the bed and slipped on his pants. On the short trip to the door, he tried to push his hair into place.

The door pushed open, but only Jonas was there, pacing outside the door. He was gnawing on the side of his thumb.

"What's wrong, Jonas?"

He whirled around. "Hey."

Michael inched forward on the cool stone floor and folded his arms across his chest. "Spill it."

"You might wanna sit down for this."

"Just tell me."

Jonas paced some more, then stopped and blurted out, "Tori knows you started the *vincolo* on her."

Michael surged toward Jonas. "Did you tell her?"

"No. I swear."

He kept pushing forward, almost up in his face. "Who the fuck told her?"

Jonas stopped, planting his feet on the floor so that he didn't tumble over a chair in the parlor. "I don't know."

"Shit!" He really didn't know. Michael could feel it. Still, someone did, and she'd never forgive him.

He started a pacing route of his own, around the chair and Jonas, to the elevator, and back. His body tensed, his fists clenched. If he didn't put his fist into something soon…. Michael screamed out his frustration and grabbed a marble statue off the table to his right. He flung it across the room and it shattered when it hit the wall.

Jonas just stared at him, shaking his head.

"What?" Michael snarled. "You have something to say? Say it."

"You've really got it bad, brother."

He let out a rickety laugh. Of course he did. He'd been bound to her for this long, watching from the shadows, and finally managed to consummate it. The relief had been spectacular. But now it was all over. Thanks to someone with a big damn mouth. "I want to know who told. Now."

"I think you already do."

"What?"

"She wouldn't confirm it, but I got the feeling that Castillo told her. Don't know how."

"Fuck." He rubbed his temple and paced again. "He would, if he could get her to listen."

"Listen, I know you've got a lot to think about, but if he told, don't you think that we should keep an eye on her?" Jonas moved closer, but not too close. "He'll probably let Damon have her."

"Yeah. You're right." Michael pushed his hands through his hair. "Dammit. If I go, she'll probably shoot me." He paced a little more. "Let me see your phone."

Jonas slid the silver cell from his pocket and handed it over.

He dialed the number to Tori's cell, put it to his ear, and started moving again. The first ring came and went.

Then another. In the silence, he felt her heart ache. She wouldn't answer and he didn't blame her.

Finally, her voice came on the third ring. *This is Tyler, leave me a message.* Beep.

Michael cleared his throat. "Tori, I know you're mad. I'm sorry. Call me and let me explain. Dammit. At least call and yell at me."

He flipped the phone shut and handed it back. "She won't call me. She's too hurt. I feel it."

Michael stood, rubbing his chest absently as Jonas put the phone away. If she didn't trust him before, there was no way it was going to happen now. The best thing he could do was just leave the poor girl alone. She deserved someone better anyway. Someone human.

"Michael?"

"Yeah." He rubbed his forehead. "What?"

"I was asking if you want me to go check on her."

Something primal surged at the thought of Jonas and her alone in her apartment—with her in a vulnerable mindset. He wanted to say no, but when his mouth opened, he said, "Yeah. Go ahead."

He moved past Jonas toward the bedroom, then shut the door quickly behind him. If he'd lost Tori, the best thing he could do was confront Castillo while there was still a connection, still strength from the bond. He might die, but he'd take that bastard out with him. Jonas could run the *cosca* when they were both gone.

* * * *

Tori grabbed a pair of black cotton panties from the top drawer of her dresser, and a white tank top, the one with the little skeleton bunny on the front, from the second. She glanced at the phone, which flashed its message indicator, but she refused to check it. Instead, she slipped into the underwear, moved to the bed, and snuggled in.

Blade darted into the room and jumped on the bed. She reached for him, but he slipped away. The cat padded to the foot of the bed, stopped, and watched the bedroom door.

"What is it, Blade?"

There was a soft footstep and the hallway creaked. Someone was in there. *Dammit.* The gun was on the dresser by the door.

She slid slowly off the side of the bed onto all fours, careful not to let it make an unnecessary sound, then crawled carefully toward the dresser. When she reached the edge, a black gloved hand pushed the door open. Her heart stopped and that sick feeling filled the pit of her stomach. She had to move quickly.

She slid up the wall and reached for the gun. Her hand grabbed the grip, but something grabbed her hand.

Stiff shirt Officer Joe Phillips swung around the doorframe. "Gotcha!"

"Let go of me." She jerked, but his grip tightened, supernaturally tight.

He yanked her out from around the dresser and pried the gun from her hand. "You're done, Tyler. This can be as ugly or clean as you want it to be."

"What the hell are you doing?"

"For a detective, you're not so smart."

Her mouth dropped open and she jerked her arm hard, trying to dislodge it. "You're with him!"

"Bingo."

"You idiot."

"Well, the way I see it," He jerked her to him so that their chests bumped. "I'll never make detective as long as you're alive."

"That's the dumbest reason I've ever heard to become a *shiavo*."

"Oh, I'm not his slave. He turned me." Joe opened his mouth and revealed long, pointed canines.

Suddenly, he leaned toward her neck. It was a rookie move, one that left him open. She dropped to her knees to break away, then rolled onto her back. With free arms, she skittered toward the bed.

"Go ahead. Run." He wiped his mouth with the back of his hand. "I kind of like that."

She jerked out a drawer from the nightstand and rummaged through for the mace. Notepad, pen, sleeping pills, but no mace.

Joe pounced, slamming her to the bed. His fangs scratched her shoulder and sent a sharp pain through her arm. She glanced down to see a slick of blood forming on the skin. She kicked at him, but he straddled her side and held her hands, which made it almost impossible to land a good one. "Get off me."

He smiled, then laid his tongue flat against the wound and licked a stroke upward.

She screamed.

Joe was suddenly in the air, flying across the room. He slammed into the far wall, knocking down pictures and cracking the drywall. Jonas appeared beside him, tensed up and fists wound as he watched the man hit the floor.

In a wide swoop, he punched something at Joe's chest. As he moved away, Tori saw a piece of wood sticking out of Joe's chest. The man was still, his eyes open and mouth gaping at an odd angle. She'd never imagined O.C.D. Joe looking so tattered before. The image was disturbing on so many levels.

Then Jonas was at her side, pulling her into his arms. "Are you okay?"

"I think so." She hugged him close, grateful for his warmth. "How did you know?"

"I didn't. I was afraid you'd been set up and started not to come here, but I couldn't get you out of my mind."

She nodded. Her heart began to slow, but her arms began to shake uncontrollably. "Thank you."

He kissed her forehead and she tried not to act surprised. "I'm just glad he didn't kill you. I don't think Michael could handle losing you."

"Would it kill him?"

Jonas leaned back. "No, but I think it would break his heart."

She smiled and pulled farther away from him.

"I know you're probably not ready, but we need to go. I'm taking you to Michael's and we'll come back to clean this up. Castillo will be looking for him soon."

Tori nodded, grabbed her jeans off the floor, and hopped into them as she moved toward the door.

Jonas grabbed her gun and keys and handed them to her. "We've got to take out Damon soon or this is going to be a disaster."

"Tomorrow night. One way or the other, this is all finished tomorrow. I can't take anymore."

* * * *

Tori glanced at her arm in the dim light from the moon that came through the passenger window of Jonas' black SUV. The wound was bleeding, and deep, but it was healing fast. Too fast. All this time she hadn't realized Michael's power in her. The way she always felt strong. She hadn't had a cold in years and a cut that should need stitches was mending itself almost so fast that she could see the skin regenerating.

"He lied to me. For a long time, Jonas."

"I know, but hon, he just wanted you to live. He didn't think you'd want the bond, and he didn't like how it happened, so he kept it a secret."

"Why didn't he just find someone else to bond and break ours?"

"Finding another mate doesn't undo the previous bond if the person is still alive."

"So, he was kind of screwed." She glanced up to see him smile at her, then looked back at the road.

"I know you're mad, but try to see the bright side."

Tori smirked. "What bright side?"

"He can kick the ass of anyone who bothers you."

She laughed. He had a point. If she'd let him, Michael would take on anyone that came after her. But, that was a lot to allow. Being Michael's mate also meant putting up with the other women who swarmed around him. "I don't think I could handle all the other women, Jonas."

He laughed. "That's partially an act to keep other *vampiro* women away, and partially for food. I think that if you truly acted like his mate, it would stop." Jonas got out of the SUV and waited. "Come on, Michael will be up soon."

She stepped out and moved around the vehicle to walk beside him toward the building. "So, are there any other deep dark secrets I need to know about?"

He laughed. "We'll never know all the secrets Michael keeps. He could work for the CIA."

"I don't think that makes me feel any better."

He smirked and motioned toward a side door. "Let's go in here."

She followed him through the door and hallway they'd taken to the limo that night. This time, though, the room on the other side was quiet and empty except for Michael's family, a group of vampire men and women of various ages, who turned to watch them walk into the room. She hugged her arms close, suddenly very aware of how many vampires surrounded her, without Michael to protect her.

Jude waved. "We wondered what happened to you."

"I had to go save Tori from that cop, Phillips, who used to come in here. Castillo turned him tonight and he attacked her." Jonas smiled down at her.

Jude pointed her finger at the group. "And you all thought she was a bad guy. I told you."

No one acknowledged the words, but she knew that somewhere underneath those cold vampire exteriors, being wrong and having it pointed out in front of a human had to sting. Tori smiled at Jude. "Thanks, I think."

Jonas tugged on her arm. "Come on. Let her get cleaned up. We've got things to do."

"Thanks." She stepped back, pulling from his grasp slowly, and grabbed the door handle. "Right now I just want a shower."

As she pushed the door open, Jonas said, "Tori?"

"Yeah?"

"Michael won't hurt you."

She smiled. There wasn't much to say back to that, so she nodded. "See ya in a bit."

Chapter Ten

TORI PUSHED the door to Michael's room open, expanding the amount of space that he'd left between it and the frame in an attempt, she assumed, to keep her from needing the key. It was silent and cast in a dim light from a lamp. Inside, the bed was tidy and a crystal vase filled with crimson roses rested on the nightstand. Everything was a reminder of him; even the air smelled like his sultry scent. It was so strong that she didn't know if she could stay and sleep in the bed they'd ma—

She forced her feet forward, moving across the room, and sat on the bed near the display. There wasn't time for this. She just needed to get the guy, stop the chaos, and get out of here. She huffed and looked at the vase. Standing against the vase was a piece of elegant folded paper, with her name inscribed on the front in an old-fashioned script handwriting. Michael's handwriting was one of the few reminders of his real age.

She picked up the rough parchment and opened it to see a note in the same scrawled writing.

> *Inamorato,*
> *I cannot apologize enough for what you must feel*
> *is a horrible deception. I assure you that my actions*

were committed purely out of the greatest respect for your life and the affection I have for you. I understand that you are angry, and so I offer my room to you and my vow never to deceive you again. I will not harass you, nor turn you away if you choose to come to me. In either case, I will protect you, as always, and hope that you will stay here until this matter is settled.

M.

Tori smiled and refolded the paper, then set it carefully back into place. If he wanted to protect her, she wasn't about to argue. She was mad, not stupid. Besides, Castillo was too strong and too smart for her. She didn't like to admit it, but that was the hard truth. Humans just didn't measure up.

She kicked off her shoes, stood, then stretched her hands above her head and arched her back in a deep bow. A yawn rolled up. She needed rest. She'd have to confront Damon soon, but if she was too tired, she'd be too weak to fight off any mental attack.

There was a loud knock at the door.

"Come in."

Jude stuck her magenta head in the door. "Can we talk?"

"Sure."

She entered, carrying a bag with a red Walgreen's label on it. She held it out as she approached. "Michael asked us to pick up a few things for you."

"Thanks." She took the bag, sat on the bed, and opened it. There was a toothbrush, toothpaste, deodorant, a hairbrush, shampoo, body wash—everything she needed but had left at home. "I really needed these. Thanks."

"He thought you might." Jude sat down beside her and the sweet, fruity scent of her perfume wafted closer. "You know, he really would take care of you if you'd let him."

"Not you, too." Tori rolled her eyes and set the bag on the floor next to her feet. "It gets really old hearing that. It's not true though. You know he runs through women."

"A meal's a meal, Tori." She picked her nails, but seemed to choose her words carefully. "I've seen him, watched him waiting for you to give him a chance. He's wrapped, girl. If he could move on, he would have by now."

"But that's just because of the bond."

"Not just. It was as bad before that. He's been watching you, protecting you." She glanced up and smiled. "He's in love with you."

"Did he send you in here?"

"No." Her voice was sharp and her head crooked sideways. "If he knew I was telling you all this he'd...he'd have my head."

"Why tell me then?"

"Because you need to know." She laughed. "If you pass this up, you're a moron. Wouldn't hurt you for the world, you know. Plus, I consider you a friend. It would be nice to have you around...like a sister."

Jude was one of the youngest, according to what she'd told Tori. Michael had found her hiding in Germany, a Jew caught in the war. He'd rescued her from an officer who had murdered her family and taken her as his own hostage, a sex toy kept in his cellar. She had a tendency to make Michael into Superman when she talked about him.

"Your life....The human limit, it's too short for you not to take advantage of this. We don't get real love twice, you know." She looked absently at the door.

"I know. I'm—Well, you know what I've been through. And now, to know that he lied to me all this time about the bond...that's just too much."

"I know, but he did that a long time ago, to save you." Jude smirked. "You should be grateful. If he'd really wanted to use you, he could have done it legally. Your life is his by our laws."

Jude was right. His lie had even been to protect her and let her keep a normal life. Still. "I know."

"You know him, Victoria. He is a gentleman, but he won't wait forever. Get over it, or watch someone else take your place."

Tori arched a brow at her.

"Yeah, I'm saying that others are interested."

Her heart disappeared and a throbbing pain took its place. Tori's heart still hurt at the thought of him with someone else, some stupid girl who'd swoon over his every move. Someone else that he would kiss…and put those long fangs into her skin. Like the girl that he'd been feeding from that night she'd tried to kill him. She'd said it was because of what Robert did, but it was more. She'd walked in on him feeding from her, biting another female. He seemed all-too-happy to do it, too. Until that moment, she'd always thought that she could trust him, even had a bit of a crush on him. That must have been why seeing it felt like such a betrayal. She'd just lost it, probably because of the bond, and attacked him.

"Are you okay?" Jude's hand landed on hers. It was warm.

"Yeah, I'm all right."

"Your hurt is so strong that even I can feel it. And I'm not very gifted where emotions are concerned." She rubbed her chest with her free hand. "You need to let go. No one's ever gonna be perfect." Jude's hand stroked hers. "Believe me, I get it. But, you don't have time to wait on this. You and Michael have to finish the bond. You'll both die if you don't."

She moved off the bed and toward the door. "If this is all that's stopping you, then you're just gonna have to take the leap…for all of us." She opened the door. "Write him a note. It will help you clear your head."

Tori nodded.

"Goodnight, hon." Jude left the room without a second glance.

Tori moved to the nightstand, grabbed the note, and found a pen in the top drawer of the stand beneath it. She flipped Michael's note over and started to write.

When she was done, she refolded the note. It wasn't as poetic as his note, but this was as good as it was getting. She didn't have the heart for mushy yet.

Tori stood and walked out the door. She turned and went to the only door with light flowing out from beneath it. It had to be where Michael was. She didn't want to see him, but if she just left the note, someone else might get it.

Tori knocked two quick raps on the door and slid the note underneath. She moved quickly down the hallway and back into the safety of the bedroom. Maybe giving him the note wasn't such a good idea after all. He might get his hopes up and there was no guarantee that she could love him or trust him. It was too late now, but she could still regret it, even if they would finish their bond soon. Maybe the bond would make her feel more secure in her decision. If it didn't, she probably wouldn't know it with all the magic floating around.

She shook her head and went for the bathroom. This was all just too much, too fast, thanks to the psycho vampire serial killer. Tori found only the shampoos and soaps that Michael used, the ones that smelled warm and masculine, in the large travertine-tiled bathroom. The environment was cold, sleek, and there was no lock on the door, but it had to do. She needed a bath, for more than just cleanliness; she needed to be alone in the warm water, to think about everything that was happening. Everything was going too fast, spinning out of control, and she had to get a hold of herself.

She slipped out of her clothes and into the oversized shower, then turned on the water. Warmth flowed out of the showerhead like a welcome rain, and she stood beneath it, letting it run down her hair and face. She closed her eyes and leaned sideways, resting her head against the wall. Her muscles twitched, as they always did when she relaxed, as if they seldom had the luxury. They probably didn't. Tori carried more than her fair share of tension, according to the chiropractor, but it came with the territory. It was part of being a cop. Having the added stress of being around the vamps wasn't helping.

Soon that would be over though. She'd catch Damon, deal with him somehow, and they'd be done. She'd go back to her normal life, the one where she didn't sleep with vampires. Michael would go back to his old life, the one that consisted of a string of Barbies that were nothing like her.

Her stomach twisted at the thought.

Damn, she'd really screwed this up. She was an idiot. All that stuff she'd promised herself went right out the window when he was around. He was her weakness. For a cop, she was acting pretty damned stupid. He just saw her as a conquest, like the others. He had to. In fact, she was probably even more of a prize because she'd put him off for so long. He probably bonded her more to have control in the department than out of any real heroism.

She covered her eyes with her hands. No, they hadn't really known each other before he bonded her, and he might have thought about using her, but who wouldn't in his position? She would have; it was only natural. Besides, she'd seen him at work. He believed in the *Alleanza* and wouldn't kill a human unless he had to. He was a good guy, if you could get past the fangs and blood part.

But then, that was the issue, wasn't it? If she got past that, and accepted their relationship, she would be going against everything she'd sworn to uphold. Then again, Jonas was right. If she didn't give in to the bond with Michael, there was a huge chance that someone else would force her into a bond.

A cool hand slipped around her waist and a very male, very hard body pressed against her back.

She jumped slightly, but it held her from turning, and Michael's voice whispered against her ear. "I'm sorry, *inamorato*."

* * * *

When she looked at him, Michael tried not to think about how beautiful she was. Instead, her feelings settled over him and brought the pain of desperation and confusion.

He used her slick shoulders to turn her slowly, then pulled her into a hug. She was soft and warm against him, and her hair tickled his nose. Then came the smell of her skin, so tempting that it made his teeth ache. It had been so long since he'd hugged someone like this. He hadn't realized that he'd missed the warmth.

She shoved against his chest.

"What?" He let go. Her heart suddenly pounded and the sound of her blood rushing through her veins filled the room. Then the scent of it made his mouth water.

"Don't think you can act sweet and I'll see you any differently."

"What are you—" He looked down at the cut on her arm. She huffed, and suddenly he felt her confusion slip into gloom.

"Why did you lie to me?"

"I didn't mean to keep it from you this long. I just didn't want to hurt you." He tried to touch her arm, but she folded them under her breasts, which were magnificent in the drizzle coming from the showerhead.

She cleared her throat and his eyes darted up to hers. She smirked. "So…making me feel this way about you and rubbing all the women in my face was better?"

"You chose not to accept me. I had to—"

"I'm not stupid. I know you see me as a piece of meat." Her anger lashed at him like a whip. The bond fanned the jealousy she naturally felt into something monstrous. She was spinning out of control.

"Victoria, please. Just listen."

"This little game isn't getting you anywhere. I just need to know who the killer is and deal with that, and then we don't have to pretend anymore."

She started to slip between him and the wall, trying to escape, but he put an arm up to block her. "Is that what you really want?"

The bitterness of her doubt permeated the air and her eyes glanced away from his, but her voice said, "Yes."

"Liar." He leaned in quickly, invaded her space and pushed his body against hers. She tried to move the other way, but he put the other arm up. Then, when she tried to duck below his arm, he had to grab her. He held her, even when she tried to squirm away. "Look at me."

She pushed against him and tried to move past. Her panic was growing uncontrollable.

"I said look at me!"

She stopped dead and rolled her eyes up to his.

"I love you, Victoria."

She let out a breath, and her shoulders sagged.

* * * *

Tori looked away from him.

"We have more in common than you think." Michael stroked the scar on her neck with his finger, and then gave it a kiss that covered her body with chills, even in the warm spray of the shower.

She closed her eyes and tried to keep the thoughts focused on how bad an idea it was to want him, but her body was beginning to betray her. The warmth between her legs was growing, tingling as she grew moist.

She took a small breath and let the words flow out. If she could be angry, she could be in control. "I'm just a conquest to you, Michael."

He stilled, then took her face in his hands and smiled down at her. "Those other women you've seen me with?"

"Yeah?"

"Warm bodies. Just food."

Something inside her relaxed slightly. Half of her wanted so desperately to hear him say that, but the other half was terrified by it. "Do they know that?"

"Some do."

"Still, some are just conquests."

"I don't think of women in those terms, and I resent the accusation—but I'll let it go for now." He kissed her softly on the corner of the mouth. "You're nothing like those women to me."

"I wish I believed you."

"So do I."

He kissed her again, but on the lips, a soft and wet kiss that drove away her ability to form solid thought. Something warm and light, like a warm glow, wrapped around her body and slid across her skin. Then she felt it—adoration. A feeling akin to reverence filled her and made her body feel like it could shed its skin and float away.

She pulled away from his kiss, breathing hard. "What is that?"

"It's how I feel about you."

She looked into his eyes and saw the mask slip away. For the moment, he was unguarded, vulnerable. She could feel the real person inside the vampire, the one who needed someone to love who would love him back. He did feel something for her, and it was—well, it was love. That was the only way to describe the feeling. If it was *trucchi*, she'd never seen it, and if it was the bond, it didn't matter. The feeling magnified what she felt and it was stronger than anything she'd ever felt for another human.

His lips came back to hers in a light brush at first, then with more force. She let her eyes slip closed and gave in to it. Her body went on autopilot. She molded against him and brought her hands to his sides. She could feel the hard muscles move as he brought his hands down to her neck.

His mouth followed, pushing her head to one side so he could kiss a trail down to her scar. His tongue slid across the slick tissue and then his mouth clamped down on top of it. Tingles rose from her feet upward, moving toward the bite as though he called some strange magic through her.

"Finish it, Michael."

She almost couldn't believe she'd said it until he stopped.

"What?"

"Finish the bond."

He looked up at her. His eyes searched hers. "We're not doing this now. You're not in any shape to—"

"Don't treat me like a child. I know what I want."

He smiled. "I would never think of you as a child. Right now, you're tired and scared. I don't want us to do this when you haven't had time to think about it."

"I know what I'm doing."

"Just think about it for the night. I want it to be just us right now. No tricks."

His lips moved back to hers and muffled out the beginning of a word, but she couldn't remember what it was. His lips slipped over hers and his tongue flicked quickly inside. She groaned and pushed forward to try to coax it back.

Someone banged at the door.

She pulled away with a gasp.

"Dammit," Michael muttered. "What is it!?"

Jonas' voice came. "It's Damon. He's upstairs harassing Christine."

"I'm coming. Go back up and keep them in the building."

Michael kissed her mouth once more, a deep and probing movement of the tongue, and then left her standing with her mouth open. He was gone so fast that she still felt him against her as she blinked her eyes open. She cut off the water and reached for a towel when she heard the bedroom door shut. His clothes were not on the floor. Damn, he was fast. How could he do that and not slip on the tile?

* * * *

The elevator doors opened and Michael caught a glimpse of Damon dragging Christine through the door toward the private bar.

"Damon, let her go," Jonas yelled.

Surely, he wasn't so ignorant. Perhaps he was such a fool as to think Castillo would protect him even in this case. If he did, Christine was in more trouble than he thought.

Michael darted through the door. Damon had Christine sprawled out on the floor and he crouched low over her with a large knife in his hand hovering over her face. They all froze.

Michael folded his arms across his chest and tried not to look impressed. "What are you doing, Damon?"

"Go back to your human whore. I have Castillo's approval and you're in my way."

Michael started forward, but Jonas grabbed his arm. "Don't you ever breathe another insult at me again or I'll have your balls."

"Castillo will end you."

"If he stands for your lawlessness, he will be killed by the council."

Damon let out a rickety laugh. "You just don't get it. They're not playing by your rules anymore. Honor really is dead."

"Leave my club before you're dead along with it."

Damon poked the knife into Christine's chest a fraction, then sliced down to make the blood flow. She screamed and Jonas started forward. Michael grabbed him. They couldn't act just yet. Damon wanted them to attack him. That would provoke Castillo and if they were gone, no one would stop his rampage.

"Stop testing me and leave, Damon."

"Okay." He leapt off Christine, grabbed her ankle, and tugged her quickly into the public bar.

"Oh, shit." Jonas muttered as they both sprang after him.

The bar was full, just after opening, and the screams let them know that humans were there to see. Jack and the others quickly began to usher people toward the exits. The police would be here soon.

People scattered like cattle as they looked around for him. Michael went right and Jonas left. Damon wouldn't make it out the door with Christine, but he might hide long enough to kill her. Michael glanced up and down, and then jumped onto the bar to see better.

"There, he's going back toward the other bar." He pointed Jonas toward the man who still dragged Christine behind him.

Michael leapt toward him, hoping to cut him off, just as the door between the bars opened. His heart sank.

* * * *

It was a good thing Tori had thought to grab her pistol as they left the house. She tucked it into the back of her pants and walked toward the elevator. She wasn't going back to that house any time soon and wouldn't want to risk anyone getting hurt trying to retrieve it.

She pressed the up button and waited for the little light to come down. She folded her arms and watched. *Someone must be up there. Maybe Michael was coming back down.*

The thing finally reached the bottom and dinged. When the doors opened, Damon flashed a twisted grin at her. He dropped what appeared to be Christine's leg on the elevator floor.

Oh, shit. She started backing away, quickly grasping for her gun.

"I've been looking for you," he said in that Scottish accent, just before he slammed into her.

It all happened so fast that she hadn't pulled her gun. Now, he had an arm around her throat, her back pinned against his chest, and she couldn't breathe. He breathed the smell of rot against her face and pulled her body up close. The psycho was actually hard from the attack. Her stomach rolled, but she swallowed it down.

He jerked her backwards into the elevator. She wanted to scream but wouldn't give him the satisfaction, even if she could have gotten enough breath to do so.

Christine's leg was beside her foot, so she kicked her hard a couple of times. Nothing. The only movement came from the blood seeping from her forehead and a cut on her chest.

He kicked the button panel hard and smashed it in. Buttons fell to the floor as wires sizzled. The light inside the elevator went out. "That should hold 'em up long enough."

Somehow, a pointed blade was suddenly at her cheek. "You're a perfect addition to my collection."

She had to keep him talking. "What collection?"

"Souls." He lifted her so she had to walk on her tiptoes and moved forward toward the hallway

She managed a muffled, "Huh?"

He shoved her against the wall and turned her so quick that she felt dizzy. "Souls. For my harem. The souls of my slaves in the afterlife. Don't tell me you've never heard of The Prophecy."

She coughed and rubbed her throat. "Yeah, it's standard, textbook psycho talk."

"Don't talk down to me, human." He grunted, grabbed her by the throat, and squeezed harder. His other hand pushed the tip of the blade into her flesh a little.

He made one long lick up her neck and then shivered against her. He grunted, then grabbed a handful of her hair. He dragged her into the common room, then toward the hallway so fast that she was stumbling and trying to keep up. "Which room is his?"

"Huh?"

"Michael's."

"Why?"

He kicked open one door to reveal a room decorated in punk band posters and black. "A fitting insult, don't you think?"

"You know Michael. He's not gonna care."

"You're his whore."

"He's got a lot of women and you know it."

He kicked open another door. This one was very girly and all pink.

She managed a laugh. "You're screwed."

"In just a few minutes. Be patient, love."

The thought made her shiver.

He dragged her to Michael's door on the other side of the hall. "Aha! A card key. Where is yours?"

"I don't have one."

He beat the little silver slot off the wall and the door budged open. He shoved it back and pushed her inside. She regained her footing just before he grabbed her. Damon flung her on the bed so hard that her head hit the headboard.

She screamed instinctively and grabbed her head.

"Beautiful scream." He was coming closer.

She shut her mouth and started off the other side of the bed, blinking through the white sparks of light that filled her vision.

He appeared in front of her and she let out a yelp.

Damon cackled. "Lay down, love. This will only hurt a lot."

She scrambled back, but he caught her by the throat and shoved her backwards, down onto the bed, cutting off her air again. He put the knife on the bed, out of her reach, and the free hand reached down the headboard. "If I know Mikey, he's got restraints in here."

She gagged and pried at his fingers as he fumbled beneath the bed. She needed Michael's strength and tried to think hard. If she could make that connection with him, she might be able to harness something, some benefit of their bond to help her, but there was nothing. No love, no fear, no anger, and no sign of him.

He let go, but in a flash, her arms yanked toward the headboard. He bound them in the same line that Michael had used on her

"There." He smiled down at her.

She kicked and tried to throw her weight to roll over.

"No, no, no. Now, for the feet."

She struggled but watched carefully as he moved to her feet. He reached down one side and found another length of rope. "Glad your honey lined the elevator to keep other *vampiro* from jumping down and bashing through. Otherwise, they'd be here to interrupt our little party."

He smiled and started toward her leg. She thrust it at him, aiming her toe squarely at his nose. When it connected, there was a loud crack and blood flew everywhere.

He screamed and fell to the floor, nursing his face. "You bitch!"

She pulled hard to free her hands, yanking and tugging, until one came loose. Her blood pounded so loud in her ears that she couldn't hear what he was saying, if he was saying anything at all. Damon was still folded over, holding his nose as she reached for her gun.

She aimed with one arm down the line of her body, at his head, and braced for the kick. As if on command, he glanced up. He rushed at her as she pulled the trigger.

His face exploded in a burst of blood and skull, but his body kept moving.

Panic shot through her. It was just like Robert, he wouldn't stop, even with half a head. She jerked the gun into a half aim and fired repeatedly as his body lurched toward her. "Just— freakin'—die!"

The body fell to the floor.

She pulled up to tug at the rope on her arm. Her hands wouldn't stop shaking so she couldn't grasp the end, and her eyes wouldn't stop glancing in his direction to make sure he didn't come back up at her like some slasher movie villain. She screamed her frustration and felt hot tears began to slide down her cheeks.

Chapter Eleven

MICHAEL DASHED through the doorway. What was left of Damon was chest down on the floor. His head was a mass of flesh and blood that leaked onto the stone. Michael smiled to himself. Tori was on the bed, covered in bits of Damon. Her hands jerked at the rope and she mumbled something. His heart ached to see her, the tough cop that no one messed with, panicked and crying. He was glad he'd blocked her emotions from taking control of him. If he hadn't, he'd probably be huddled in a corner somewhere crying, too.

He walked around behind her, careful not to startle her. His arms went around her and quickly snapped the rope. She looked up and then leapt into his arms.

Jonas whistled. "She destroyed him."

He glanced back to see the group huddled in the doorway.

"Leave us." Michael couldn't stop his voice from sounding a little harsher than necessary. "Jonas, pick a crew to clean this up while I get her cleaned up. Everyone else upstairs."

Tori was shaking in his arms, her body rocking with sobs that she fought to hold back. When the others left, she let the tears flow. He pulled her hard against his chest. He should have been just a little faster, just like the last time. He would have defended anyone against that monster, but Tori required more. He should have gotten to kill Damon himself, the sorry bastard. With all that she'd been through, she shouldn't have had to deal with it herself.

He scooped her up in his arms. For the first time she felt fragile, like a child. She buried her head against his shoulder as he carried her into the bathroom and shut the door.

When he sat her down on the counter, she looked up at him with red, tear-filled eyes. "I'm sorry."

He pushed the matted hair away from her face. "Why?"

"I just killed him and screwed it all up. Castillo's going to come after us."

"He would anyway."

"And I cried in front of your family, like a kid. I just couldn't stop, and—"

"Don't ever apologize for crying in front of them." He kissed her on the forehead. "They'll just be less afraid of you now."

When he laughed, she smiled a little.

"You're my *amante*. Anything you do in front of them is appropriate."

She nodded.

"Now we've got to get you cleaned up. I'll have to deal with Castillo quickly. He'll know Damon's gone." Since her shirt was ruined, he ripped it off and tossed it into the trash. "Take those off and I'll start the water."

* * * *

She stripped down and stood watching as he carefully set the shower temperature. Bits of blood and flesh covered her, but she tried not to think about it. Instead, she needed to focus on what was coming at them; one pissed off *Vampiro padrone*.

"Get in. I'll get you some more clothes."

She nodded and stepped into the warm shower. Although taking a long soak would have been nice, she jumped straight to shampooing and scrubbing. She had to scrub twice as hard to make sure everything was gone, but no matter how clean it looked, she still felt dirty, as though part of Damon had seeped into her skin from his blood.

Michael really wasn't like the rest of them. Damon, Castillo, and even Robert were bad people to start with. Becoming vampires didn't change that, it just made it more obvious. Michael had been a warrior, a respected and chivalrous Roman, from what she'd heard from the others. He'd had plenty of time to bed other women and coax them into bonds, but from what she knew Tori was the only one he'd carried on a relationship with of any sort in recent years. Maybe being his *amante* wasn't such a bad thing after all; it very much resembled being his wife.

The thought made her smile.

"Here are your clothes."

She jumped at the sound of his voice, but smiled at Michael when he peered around the glass door. He'd never fussed over her so much, and it was cute.

"So, you're done?"

"Yeah."

"I'll get a towel."

She turned the tap off, stepped out onto the soft rug in front of the shower, and saw him standing close to the bedroom door.

Michael turned back and just looked at her for a moment. He moved closer and opened the towel. His eyes glanced to hers, then back to her body quickly, trying to be respectful, but still obviously enjoying the view.

Tori stepped forward and let him wrap her in it. His hands moved slowly as they pushed the soft cotton against her, soaking up the water. She didn't look down to watch though;

she stayed locked on his eyes. She tried to will him to feel her emotions—how her heart swelled with the thought of being his lover and *amante*.

"Stop blocking me," he whispered.

She felt the walls slide away and the connection between them opened again. He breathed in hard, but she didn't stop. Her hands slid up his shirt and around his neck. She moved forward, dodging his attempt to kiss her, and took his earlobe between her lips. She nibbled softly and felt him harden against her.

Tori released the bit of skin and whispered, "I'm not afraid of you anymore."

He groaned and squeezed her tight.

"I want to finish it, to be your *amante*."

He pulled back and looked down at her as his hands worked nervously up and down her back.

She felt his disbelief, then concern, and finally pride. "I love you, Michael."

"There's no going back."

"I know."

She jumped back as he took her mouth in a hungry kiss. She heard the fall of fabric as he tossed the towel onto the floor behind her, but her brain was too focused on his talented mouth to care.

Michael's hands worked down her sides to grasp her butt, then pulled her up so that she could wrap her legs around his waist. He stroked her skin firmly but with all the reverence of someone touching his new child.

She didn't pull away as he lowered them to the floor and laid her out on the towels. But when he pulled back from the kiss, she opened her eyes. "What is it?"

He buried his head against her nape and began to kiss her softly. "Say it again."

She smiled and felt her heart begin to swell. He had heard her. "I love you, Michael."

"I wish we had more time." He pressed his weight against her in long strokes that sparked her arousal.

"But we don't." She arched toward him, baring her neck to him and offering herself in every way. Her hands stroked up his back and felt the muscles rolling under the skin as he shifted himself back and forth.

Michael let out a low, rumbling growl and scratched a tooth across her skin. Her body jolted and he gripped her hard. He sucked softly at her neck while she fumbled to open his pants. In a short moment, he was out, and the hot tip of his cock pressed against her slick skin.

Tori pressed up against him, but he pushed her back against the floor when he thrust forward. Her heart pounded and her nipples ached. She was so close, even without the added benefit of penetration.

With a quick shift in weight, he flipped them so that she was on top, staring down at him lying on the towels and rug. He propped up on one elbow and grabbed a handful of her hair with the other hand. "Come here, *amante.*"

He pulled her gently but firmly down to his mouth and onto his body. She gasped as his mouth locked onto hers again and his body filled hers. She ground her hips slowly against him, careful not to push too hard or deep. The one hand she used to hold herself up began to shake as a swell of pleasure rode through her. Her arm gave way and she fell against him.

Michael released her neck and sat them both up. She tried to watch him swirl his tongue around her nipple, but her eyes fluttered shut. She could feel his teeth teasing, pinching softly at her flesh, forcing another wave.

His hand reached for her hair again and he pulled her down hard onto him. The pain and pleasure mix made her shudder against him. He moaned with her and then arched her neck toward his mouth.

The start of a dazzling orgasm filled her body just as the tips of his teeth sank into her neck. The sensation magnified everything, along with their connection, and the world became one pounding freefall. There was none of the fear she'd expected, only an intense need to be one with him, to stay with him and make him her own.

Michael was holding her and had managed somehow to move her back under him. He licked one long stroke up her neck as he spoke in words she didn't understand—Italian, maybe. It sounded like the dream, but it didn't matter.

She opened her eyes and tried to focus on him.

"*Amante*, kiss me. Take what I offer you, a long life under my protection." He kissed the corner of her mouth. "In exchange for your trust, take my protection and power."

She felt his mouth again, pressing on hers softly, but forcefully. When his hand stroked her neck, she opened for him. His tongue slipped inside and stroked hers, giving her warm, copper-flavored draws of his blood.

Tori swallowed. Something inside of her clawed toward the surface whenever he kissed her. It stretched and expanded until it filled every inch of her.

She tried to breathe, but couldn't pull herself away. Her hands gripped his sides as some deep, animalistic part of her tried to drink him down. She felt him pulling her tighter and heard his groan, which only made her want to eat him even more.

Then it happened. That link between them that had always been there exploded. She felt him. No, she felt what it was to be him, to see her through his eyes. She saw how he'd bound her the first time, felt the need for her night after night and the devastation of her trying to kill him and leaving for so long. She saw, through Michael's eyes, how Jonas looked at her and knew that he wanted her too, but didn't pursue it because of his loyalty. She felt the anxiety of knowing that she, his lover, was trapped in that room with Damon, and then the joy of hearing her say she loved him. In one quick flash, she knew how he truly felt about her and how long he'd struggled with it.

And then it was gone.

Something pulled Tori back down the tube of their connection. The weight of her own body felt somehow strange and foreign until Michael pulled her closer and she could feel their hearts beating in time and their breath coming and going together. Her eyes blinked open and she saw him smiling at her. There were no words to say, no need to talk. She knew all she needed to know.

He gave her another quick kiss and rolled them both onto their sides, facing each other.

She burrowed closer into the space between his arm and shoulder. Her eyelids drooped until they closed. For the first time in a long while, her entire body was relaxed and her muscles weren't twitching. Her heart was ready to get up and prepare for the fight with Castillo, but her body was too tired.

"We need to go." Michael brushed his fingers over her cheek.

"Just let me rest for a few minutes."

He chuckled. "We can't sleep, *amante*. He could be here at any moment."

"Please."

"Five minutes." His lips gave hers a quick touch. "And then we go."

* * * *

Tori felt something along her skin, like tiny bugs crawling and nipping at her. She had the faintest hint of memory, as if she'd felt this before. Something akin to spiders along the flesh.

Her eyes flew open. "What is that?"

Michael was pulling on a button-down shirt. "Get dressed."

She sat up and started to pull on the T-shirt Michael had laid on the counter. Something was wrong. Very wrong. "Michael, what's going on?"

"Castillo."

The feeling grew stronger as she tugged on a pair of jeans that were a little too big. They must have been Jude's or one of the other women's.

"Michael, we've got trouble." Jonas called from the hall, just before Castillo's power flooded the room. "Get out here."

He grabbed Tori's hand and tugged her through the bedroom and into the common room, her bare feet slapping on the cold floor. They turned the corner and moved into the large room just in time to see Castillo emerging from a set of stairs hidden by what Tori had always assumed was a closet door. Jonas turned toward him, standing as a barricade between his friend and his city's *padrone*.

Castillo looked every bit the Spanish model that he had looked in the alley. His neatly pressed slacks and open-collar shirt looked as though he'd put them on just for this visit. He looked professional and cold until his voice echoed through the room. "Where is my child?"

Michael moved to stand between Castillo and Jonas. "Dead."

"Where?" The *padrone* pushed past Michael and headed down the hall.

"In my chamber. He came here and attacked my *amante*— in my own room." He followed, but kept a little distance behind Castillo.

He whirled on Michael. "You had no right to kill him."

"Under the *Alleanza*, I do."

"Don't quote the law to me, *leggero*."

It was an insult and Tori felt his anger flash, but he didn't let it show to the others. Instead, Michael said, "With all due respect, *Padrone*, Damon has been breaking our laws for months. He murdered humans needlessly and garnered human attention. My *amante* is the detective who was charged with his capture."

"And you helped her?" The muscles in Castillo's jaws flexed. "You betrayed our kind."

"No, I upheld the *Alleanza* while you betrayed us."

Castillo held out his hand and continued his hard stare at Michael. "Give her to me and I will be lenient with you, *fratello*. There is no *vincolo* between you. You haven't finished her and I claim her as mine."

"No." Michael let himself smile.

Victoria shook her head. If Michael was smiling, it couldn't be good. Either he was trying to pick a fight, or he wasn't as smart as she'd given him credit for. In any case, she was surprised that Castillo couldn't feel their bond. That could only happen if Michael wasn't part of his line. Interesting.

"Michael, I can force you."

"She has done nothing wrong and broke no law. I won't allow you to take her."

"Nor will I," Jonas added, stepping up beside his leader.

Castillo's henchmen poured down the stairway and surrounded the group. "You betray me again? You ungrateful little *shiavo*." The *padrone* moved closer, clenching his fists. "Michael, you are my favorite, but you can be replaced."

She watched the two carefully tossing words at each other. *Shiavo* was an interesting choice of insults. Had he been a slave to Castillo at some point? It would explain some of Michael's more interesting quirks. If he had been a blood slave, he must have been tortured in the process. Castillo didn't seem the kind to pass up the opportunity to break someone who had a strong spirit. She shivered at the thought.

Michael arched a brow at her, as though he'd heard the thought, but said, "I refuse to give her to you."

The man let out a roar, and the vampires in the room bowed forward as if someone sucker-punched them all simultaneously. Tori's head began to pound with a sharp ringing that pierced her brain. She covered her ears just as Castillo reached toward her.

Michael grabbed the man's wrist.

In an instant, Castillo swung out a dagger and slammed it into Michael's chest.

He froze on the spot, eyes wide, and collapsed.

Chapter Twelve

TORI GASPED in a breath and grabbed her chest. Pain poured from the void between her ribs. The white, blaring throb made her arms and legs, even her teeth, ache. Her knees buckled and she went down. Apparently, even pain passed through their connection.

As if he'd heard the thought, Jonas was suddenly at Michael's side.

Michael's voice boomed through her mind. *No. Don't provoke him.*

Jonas stopped in mid-step. There was a long pause and then Michael's voice came back again, *Block the connection between us, Tori.*

She struggled to breathe in against the weight of pain in her chest, and then tried to concentrate on Michael and their tie. She pushed away from him, from the power that came with him. The hum between them faded slowly, and she pushed away, inch by inch, until she could breathe. Then she pushed again. The pain faded to an uncomfortable sting in her heart.

She didn't try to stand. Instead, she sat there on her knees, shaking as she slowed her breathing. She had to stall, to think of something to help Michael.

"Don't touch him. No one touches him until I leave this building." Castillo reached for Tori again. "That is silver in his chest. Come with me now, or he dies. It's your choice and makes no difference to me."

Jonas started to move between them, but Tori held out her arm. He gave her a look of confusion mixed with sadness.

He would understand. He understood now, even though he didn't want to. If she stayed, they'd all die. Castillo was just crazy enough to risk the elders' wrath for his revenge. If she left, and Michael was right about their bond giving him enough power to stop Castillo, then they'd all have a chance.

So, she smiled and nodded her submission to Castillo.

"Smart girl. Perhaps I won't kill you." He grabbed her wrist and yanked her toward him. "He didn't have my permission to bring you over, and I should have taken you then, but it may work for the best. You'll replace Damon nicely."

"What?" Tori arched a brow at him. She was prepared to die, but taking any place at Castillo's side, especially as his lover, was out of the question.

"Castillo." Jonas surged forward and Castillo's people moved toward him. "She didn't know. She's not one of us!"

"Enough!"

"No." Jonas grabbed Tori's other hand.

Stop him. Michael's voice rang in her head. He didn't have to explain; in a flash, she knew what to do. Michael didn't so much tell her in words as give her ideas. It had to be quick, believable, and earn Castillo's trust.

She whirled toward him, shoved him away, and yelled. "Don't, Jonas. Michael betrayed me. Now, I want a real master for a change."

As she stared into Jonas' eyes, his mouth dropped open. She wanted to take the words back, but it was working, she could feel it somehow through Michael. Jonas was his, one of his line.

With the power Michael possessed for *trucchi*, she threw her will at him and forced the vampire to stay perfectly still. He put up less of a fight than she'd expected, but it wouldn't have mattered. Jonas simply wasn't strong enough to go against Michael, and now, by extension—her.

"You made your point. They won't follow." Castillo gripped her shoulder. "Now, let us leave."

She swallowed back the twinge of fear that came when Castillo took her hand. Then she went numb as he pulled her toward the doorway. Inside her own mind, she whispered, *Please don't let him keep me.*

"Don't, Tori." Jonas muttered behind them.

She breathed out hard. They'd come, Michael would fight. Castillo might be stronger. He was, after all, Michael's elder and the *padrone*. Her heart sank at the thought. "And don't let him come after me."

Castillo tugged her up the stairs, then through the private bar. Part of her wanted one of Michael's *cosca*, someone to stop him, or at least try, but she knew it would only mean their death. No one moved. Instead, they watched silently. She wanted to scream and run back, but that would mean Michael's death, and probably hers. She pushed forward and made it quietly through the public bar, up the stairs, and out the front doors with only the glares of men and women to argue for her freedom.

Near the coat check, Jude stood with an older man that Tori didn't recognize. She cried silently. It made Tori realize that she'd never known, until now, that vampires didn't cry pink, bloodstained tears.

Tori smiled at her. "It's okay."

The girl turned her back, buried her face in the man's chest.

At the door, Gregory and Blane refused to open the door or get out of the way. Castillo had to shove hard to move them. Deep inside where the monster couldn't see her betrayal, she smiled. If she survived, she'd have to give them both a big hug.

A long, black limo that looked too much like a hearse waited for them. She'd probably bargained for her own death. The best she could hope for was to become another of Castillo's demented human toys. Would she keep the bond with Michael? If Castillo was strong enough, she might not even remember who Michael was when he was through with his sick initiation. Plenty of humans went insane with the beginnings of the bond. If Castillo were to break theirs, he'd have to work some very strong *trucchi*. She just didn't know if she had the strength left to keep fighting.

As they approached, she felt Michael revive as though she'd felt her own lungs fill with a sudden gasp of breath. She couldn't help but smile.

His anger came next in a scalding wave that took her breath away. Castillo must have felt it too because he grabbed her and tossed her the dark automobile. She bounced across the seat and landed against a hunk of muscle. It grabbed Tori by the upper arm. She looked up to see a man in a leather mask sneering at her. She pushed at him, but he laughed and jerked the shirt off her shoulder.

Before she could strike him again, the monster sank his teeth into her shoulder. She screamed as the teeth ground into her skin and broke through with a dull pop. He pulled hard against her, gorging himself on blood. There was no sex appeal in his bite. It was only dull, throbbing pain.

When she shoved him, he bit harder. She screamed again. If she pulled, he would take muscle away with him. Still, she considered it, but it didn't matter. The lights around them from the street lamps began to fade, and darkness took over.

Chapter Thirteen

THE PAIN of having the silver pulled from Michael's chest radiated throughout his torso and pinged off his ribs, but there was something else. His heart was beating, effortlessly. Good. He'd heal faster this way. It must be the bond.

The bond. He couldn't feel Tori anywhere. He didn't sense anything other than the slight buzz in his mind that was their connection. If the connection remained, she had to be alive. She was unconscious. *That bastard hurt her.*

"Michael, are you okay?"

He opened his eyes. Jonas squatted beside him holding the dagger. He tried to get up, but his arms felt limp. He struggled to sit, but even that made him feel old and weak. When he jumped to his feet, he let out a roar of frustration.

Jonas leapt backward, then forward in time to catch Michael on his fall back toward the floor.

"You need blood. The silver's still poisoning your system."

Michael grabbed Jonas' arm and tried to steady himself against the spinning room. "I've got to stop him."

"It's too late. They're gone and Tori held me in the *reverie* until she left. I'm guessing that you found time to complete the *vincolo* in all of this."

He tried to keep standing but his knees were weak.

When they caved, Jonas wrapped an arm around him and dragged him the short distance to the couch. "You're not going anywhere right now. I promised I'd stop you. I won't let her die either." Michael tried to crawl off the couch, but Jonas pushed him back down.

He looked down to see dark blood tainting his veins, running outward from the wound in his chest. "Hurry."

"We're not strong enough. You've got to be healthy to go after them." Jonas slashed his wrist with the dagger and held it out. "I'd rather not be the Slurpee in this one, but my blood is as strong as you're going to get here."

There wasn't time to argue. Michael's skin was crawling with the itchy bugs of the allergic reaction to silver. He nodded and took the wrist in a bite that was faster than he meant. Jonas flinched. The blood flowed warm and thick into his mouth. After a few swallows, he could feel it radiating down toward the wound, driving the itch back toward its starting point.

He concentrated on the injury and drank again. This time he felt the wound stitch itself together.

He released the wrist and sat up quickly. The room began to spin.

"You can't leave that fast." Jonas reached for him.

He shoved the hand away. "Get out of my way."

"You're one stubborn ass, you know it? If you go after them, you're going to die and leave us all with Castillo." Jonas' jaw flexed back and forth. It was the first time in a very long time that Michael had seen him worry. "Tomorrow night we'll all go after her, but tonight you rest. She'll be alive. Castillo's planning to keep her."

Michael growled and it made his brain vibrate. "Wake me in three hours."

"That's not enough time."

"I mean it, Jonas."

"I will." Jonas gave him a slight nod of submission. "And call in the clans. Tonight, we'll take the city."

* * * *

Tori heard voices coming closer. Beneath her body lay the cold stones of the floor. She tried to open her eyes. The lids wouldn't budge. She was tired and the cold went deeper than her skin. Her cold felt like it would shake if it had the strength.

A door opened somewhere to her left and she heard footsteps coming closer. One set thudded heavily and the other sound was faster with sharp clicks; a woman. They stopped close to her head and then a sharp point nudged her shoulder hard.

"You killed her, you bloody moron." The woman's voice carried with it a British accent.

A sharp point of the heel pressed into her shoulder. Tori tried to yell *Stop*, but her mouth wouldn't open. Instead, a soft groan came from her throat.

"Oh." The woman giggled.

"See." The man's deep voice fit Mr. Leather perfectly. "I didn't."

"Close enough. Castillo wants her ready for bonding."

Tori tried to scream, but the best she could do was groan again.

"Hold her still while I feed her," the woman said.

A strong arm jerked her up so hard that her spine cracked. Her back pressed against a very large male form, covered in leather. It was Mr. Leatherface from the car, and he put an arm around her chest to hold her tight to him.

"Won't that bond her?" Leather grunted.

"She doesn't need enough to bond her. Only a bit."

Something pushed Tori's head back and cold hands opened her mouth. Warm tinny liquid pooled on her tongue, then slid down her throat. Immediately it began to absorb into her throat, burning and expanding. She swallowed it down weakly, and when it hit her stomach, it exploded so hard that her body jolted. Her body took in a deep gulp of air and her eyes flew open to see the sinister stone room. It actually looked more like a dungeon, complete with shackles and a nude and bloodied woman huddled in the corner. Chains led from her arms to a loop in the wall.

"Ah, there she is." The woman smiled and wiped the corner of Tori's mouth. She was an attractive brunette with silky hair and a cute upturned nose. A quick glance down and it was obvious that someone invested a lot of money in silicone. "Put her down, Brom."

Tori jerked away as he let her go. She glared up at him. *He almost killed me.* She swung hard and landed a punch right in his jaw. "Greedy bastard."

He raised his hand and the woman caught his wrist. Brom growled. "But, Anne. She hit me."

"Let it go. She's a human." She released him and turned to Tori again. "Castillo is expecting your best behavior. We have a visitor tonight and misbehavior will be punished."

"Whoop-dee friggin' do."

"Don't test me." The woman edged close to her face and her pupils dilated slowly as power began to swirl around them like a winter wind. "There is a lot I can do to you without killing you, especially with that little tie Michael has with you."

Tori nodded.

The woman walked out the old wooden door in the corner. Brom pushed her and she followed into a hallway.

It wasn't just any hallway. She'd seen it before. It was the one that they'd walked through on the way to the private room at *The Scene*. Through the next door, they entered the vampire club area. It looked the same as the night she and Michael made their visit, but with more patrons, more leather, and even more fantasies playing out in public view. The room carried the scent of blood and bleach again, but this time the blood didn't smell sickening. This time, it made her stomach growl.

On the small stage, three women in sheer belly-dancer costumes gyrated to an intoxicating drumbeat. Their hips rotated in circles as their arms stroked the air in sensual movements like writhing snakes. Guests watched the women as they sped up and slowed with vampire precision in a dance that was as frightening as it was exotic.

Brom pushed her forward once and she stumbled. She caught up with the woman just as she approached a banquet table that comfortably held Castillo, clad in a classic black tuxedo for the occasion, and a girl beside him in a red leather sheath dress, both just left of the center. To the right sat a Middle Eastern man with shoulder-length dark waves and a Vandyke beard. Even without *trucchi*, he was attractive, and when he smiled, she couldn't look away. Beside him was a young girl, too young to be his bride, dressed in elaborate robes and a fancy veil. Next to her sat a man in his early thirties who must have been his brother or some other genetic relative.

"Madame, we have brought your *cane*."

"Thank you, Anne." Castillo smiled up at Tori.

His fangs showed more than she'd ever seen Michael's. They were long and sleek with razor tips. Maybe he'd hidden them from her all this time? She hoped not, but somehow the thought of him walking around with those two tiny white daggers in his mouth made him seem more dangerous.

Castillo motioned to a chair on his left behind the towering crimson rose centerpiece. "Sit." Tori moved to sit in the chair as he continued to speak. "Khalil, this one will be my newest *sorella*. Her name is Victoria and she is a detective with our local police department."

Tori tried not to react to the thousands of alarms going off inside her body. Instead, she sat still between the city's *padrone* and his visitor. She would not be Castillo's newest progeny. Death or not, she wouldn't be turned into a vampire.

"You don't find that a risky choice?" Khalil eyed her carefully.

"Her dear fiancé was turned some time ago and she learned of our kind when he attacked her, and she has upheld our *Alleanza*."

"Why was her memory not removed?"

"She handled the information well and she proved to be a useful ally."

"Yes, I can see how, but did the council know of your decision?"

"Of course."

He gave Tori a look that said he didn't believe it. "And you welcome this?"

Castillo laughed. "Of course she does."

Tori looked away. She wasn't going to make it any harder on Michael than it had to be. Her time as their hostage would be hard enough without Castillo's added chastisement over his stolen bond. She might even survive long enough to get away if she didn't piss him off.

People began to clap around them. The dancers moved to the table for one last bow in front of Khalil, who offered them a gracious standing ovation.

Castillo stood, too. "Thank you for your dance, sisters. You have proved your talents once again."

They smiled at Khalil, then hurried through a side door, giggling as they went.

"And now, I have one more gift for you as we retire to our meeting. This one I arranged especially for Khamar. If you'll follow me."

The younger man flashed an eager smile. They followed Castillo as he moved around the corner of the table toward the private rooms. Tori remained in the chair, watching them, and hoping that they'd overlook her in the rush to impress the new guy.

Khalil leaned down and whispered toward her. "I don't believe he intends you to stay here." He offered his hand.

She didn't take it, but slid out of the chair.

Khalil walked beside her as she sluggishly followed. "You must be a very strong woman."

"Why?"

"You have risen to a powerful position in our domain." She nodded and let him hold the door open for her as he continued. "Most would have either been killed or locked away in an asylum in your position."

She laughed, partially because she had to be crazy to go willingly with Castillo, and partially because he was right. "I'm not sure I shouldn't be locked up right now."

He laughed with her and followed close as they went down the same hallway again. "I share your sentiment, but two thousand years has this effect on the mind."

She looked at him. Two thousand years? He didn't look more than his late thirties, but he was the oldest vampire she'd ever met, much older than Michael. To have so much power, he must have been hiding it all along.

"Don't look so surprised."

"I just didn't expect you to be that old."

"Most don't."

"In here, please." Castillo motioned them inside and shot a warning look to Tori as they passed.

Tori smiled and gave him a wink that made his brow arch high. He didn't know what she was doing and didn't trust her. Good. He shouldn't. If there was a way to have his head served up on a platter by the older vampire, who was surely his superior, she would do it—no matter what it was. It might just save them all.

Chapter Fourteen

INSIDE THE large stone room, in front of a line of three couches stood a small and fragile-looking girl, with long blonde hair; the one from the dungeon. The girl cowered against the wall like a beaten dog. Brom towered over her holding a chain that went from the collar on her neck to the leather strap in his hand. With his free hand, the man whipped a black sheet off a small table, revealing a number of blades, paddles, whips, and other frightening tools.

Khamar rubbed his hands together and smiled. Brom handed the end of the chain to Castillo and folded his huge arms across his chest.

"Khamar, this is my gift to you. My youngest *shiava* is yours to keep. She is tested, but not broken."

He took the chain. "Thank you. This is a most generous gift."

Khalil leaned against the wall near the entrance. He whispered, "Try to remember where you are."

She started to look at him, then glanced back in time to see Castillo and Khamar smile at each other wickedly. Castillo added, "Please, let us enjoy your first test of the girl to be sure she will suit your needs."

He gave the younger brother a shallow bow, and then walked to the girl. He jerked her forward so that she fell on her face. She glanced up with a bloody lip. Khamar smirked. "You will address me as master. Understood?"

The girl nodded.

He jerked her to her knees and backhanded her so hard that her head snapped sideways. Tori started forward and Khalil grabbed her arm. When she looked back, he shook his head.

The girl's scream cut through the room and Tori glanced over to see her scrambling backward. Khamar stalked toward her with fangs bared and a curved blade in his hands.

"Don't. Please. Master, please."

The predator's power flashed through the room and cut at the skin like paper. Tori glanced down at her arm to make sure she wasn't bleeding, then back again. The girl screamed and kicked at him wildly with her feet. The man hissed at her and grabbed her ankle.

Tori flinched and jerked again toward the girl.

Khalil turned her toward him. "Perhaps it is best that you look at me, Detective."

"Make him stop. I can't just stand here and watch this."

"It appears that you have no choice. This is their way." He leaned forward and whispered, "Watch. This is Castillo's way, too. Learn from this, if you want to survive."

The girl screamed again and Tori looked back at them. Khamar was on hands and knees over the girl, snapping at her each time she stopped screaming. She pushed at him and it made him cackle. He fed on her fear like cake and begged for more.

The girl held her hand out to Tori and screamed, "Help me. You're not like them. I see it. Please."

"Do not turn away from me, *shiava*." The man put the blade to the mound of her breast and cut a long, thin slice. The girl wailed again. Khamar laughed.

If this was how Castillo was going to be, then Tori would end it herself. She wasn't going to let them torture her for the rest of her life only to turn her and continue for eternity. She wouldn't beg, or scream. She'd die before she was a quivering hunk of skin on the floor, bleeding for their entertainment.

The monster leaned back and let the girl crawl across the floor, to the wall, screaming. He smiled and twirled his blade. "I do it, anyway. Over and over until you enjoy it."

The girl screamed until her breath ran out, inhaled, and screamed again. Tori wanted to scream, too, but she covered her ears. Somehow, watching the two of them in the horrific scene, it was clear that Khamar was just as scary as Castillo. Jonas had been right. Michael wasn't like him. She should have bonded with him long ago and helped him end their little psycho reign.

Khamar crooked a finger at the girl. "Come here and let us finish what we've started."

"No, run from him, please," Castillo said.

The girl stood and ran to Tori. "Help me."

That was it. She couldn't stand here and watch this. No one was coming to help her, if Jonas kept his promise. They were on their own and it was down to one thing. It was better to die helping the girl than to live waiting for her turn.

* * * *

Michael had been dreaming about something horrible, but it was gone. Still, the fear lingered like the tang of sour candy on his tongue. He couldn't remember everything, but there'd been a man. He was torturing a woman. Screams. God help them all if it had been real. If they hurt her, he'd drain them all dry.

Someone was talking. Michael opened his eyes. It took a moment for his body to pull itself into the real world. Jonas was standing over him. He was dressed in black clothes that looked like tactical gear, which could only mean that he'd been shopping on the Internet again. The *fratello* was just slender enough to fool the others into thinking he was weak, but he was probably the most dangerous of all of them.

Jonas smiled. "Time to go. I let you sleep until everyone arrived. They're ready, even the Serpentine. They're ready to see Castillo go."

"Really?" The Serpentine—a *vampiro* family who specialized in shaved heads and tattoos—didn't trust anyone, especially other *vampiro*. Their help always came with a steep price.

Jonas shifted a little. "Well, I had to promise most of them that if they helped you take out Castillo, you'd hear out their ideas, like a democracy."

"What?!" Michael shook his head. "That will never work. The *padrones* won't support that." He ran his hands through his hair. "I guess we'll have to worry about it later. We need them."

Jonas nodded, and when he sat up, his friend put a large black pistol in his hand. Michael arched a brow at him. He didn't need a pistol. In fact, he might as well bring a squirt gun. It would probably be just as effective.

"In case you need a backup. It's loaded with glow rounds."

"Good idea." He stood and tucked it in the back of his pants. The others always used what they called glow rounds, which were actually loaded with phosphorous, if they needed an underhanded advantage. He didn't like it, but now wasn't the time to be too proud. "Does everyone know the plan?"

Michael grabbed a black wife-beater shirt from the end of the bed, the one he'd laid out before he went to sleep, and slipped it over his head. It was tight and didn't look like anything else in his wardrobe, but it was great for fighting.

"Yep. Just like you said. We go in hard and fast. Take them all out." Jonas moved toward the door. "Oh, Marcus said Castillo had a visitor tonight. Someone important, he thought."

"The more the merrier. Do we have anyone inside?" Michael worked fast to put on and lace up his black boots. They were old and dingy, but he'd worn them to hunt and kill for years. He wasn't about to stop now.

"We've sent a few in just to make sure no one catches on before we get there." Jonas slipped on a pair of dark shades. "Hopefully, they'll never know what hit them."

"Let's go."

* * * *

"Leave her alone." Tori tucked the girl behind her. She felt Michael somewhere deep in her mind and couldn't stop the smile that spread her lips wide. *I love you*, she thought.

"Step away from her." Khamar waved the knife at her. "You are not mine to train, human, but I will train you—and break you."

"No." The girl screamed.

"You have my permission to teach her a lesson, Khamar."

"Thank you." He smiled.

Her stomach knotted. Immediately she felt Michael's reaction like boiling anger on her brain. He pushed at her brain, questioned her location, and worried, all without words. She wanted to answer it, but there was too large a chance that he would respond. He couldn't be foolish enough to come after her, even though she'd love to see him come barging in and kill all of them in one swoop of power.

Khamar's power lashed out again, but this time she accidentally glanced at him. Her eyes didn't close quickly enough to avoid his attempt to *enthrall* her. She fell forward in her mind, into the darkness of his power. Her mind began to swim like when she'd had too many margaritas and walked into the wall at the Halloween party at *The Fallen*.

The weight in her hand caused her to look down. She was holding something. She glanced down to see the girl's wrist and followed its line up to see her mouth open again, screaming something. Her body began to walk toward him, even as she willed it to still. Panic screamed through her. She tried to keep her foot planted on the floor, but it lifted and moved toward him. When she reached out for Michael again, their link was gone.

No, she screamed silently. *I'm not doing this.*

Oh, but you are, Khamar's voice said in her mind. *Now give her to me.*

She tossed the girl at him, and then fell to the floor on folded knees. Her hands grabbed the girl's wrists and held them to the floor while Khamar knelt between her flailing legs. The girl screamed pleas at her, but she wasn't strong enough to honor them. She didn't want to hold her. She wasn't a monster like them, but she couldn't stop. She couldn't even stop the tears that began to flow down her cheeks.

Khamar's blade came up to the girl's abdomen and slashed a K into the flesh. It gaped open, revealing the pinkish meat underneath. Her stomach turned somersaults. It wouldn't kill her, but she'd probably have his initial in her for life.

"You're next," Khamar said.

Fuck you, she thought as she tried hard to make her hands let go. Still, they stuck in their place.

Don't use such language to me, cane. You are under my rule with your dominatore's blessing. It is wise for you to obey.

I'm not scared of you.

No? Suddenly she was dragging the girl. She sat upright and pushed her toward Khamar, who smiled. He yanked the girl's neck to one side and plunged his teeth into the soft flesh of her neck. His eyes locked on Tori, then rolled upward behind dark lashes as he drank.

I've seen teeth before. Not impressed.

He blinked back to her and dropped the pale girl to the side.

When he gave a questioning glance to Castillo, he returned a nod. His face turned back with a wicked grin. His arms worked in catlike moves as he climbed over the girl toward her. She wanted to run, but nothing would move. She kicked and fought and screamed inside, but her entire form was motionless.

When Khamar's hand wrapped around her wrist, his mind let go.

In a rush, Tori regained control. Without thinking, she punched him hard in the face, and blood oozed from the corner of his mouth. He smiled, grabbed a handful of her hair, and thrust her to the ground in front of him. He mounted her waist and pinned her hands above her head. His weight pressed her bones into the floor. She was face to face with him, but was no closer to stopping him than before.

"Careful brother, this is not your *shiava*." Khalil moved closer.

With his free hand, the man flipped the knife carelessly, only a few inches from her face. "I hope you don't faint easily."

* * * *

Michael approached *The Scene*'s front door but it didn't open. He groaned, but before he could complain, two of the Serpentine *fratellos* ripped the door off its hinges. He smirked. So much for the silent entry.

Jonas led the way in and, to Michael's surprise, there were no screams. Gregory, Blane, Danny, and the others fell in behind him. They were all wound tight and ready for a fight. Apparently, Michael was the only one of his own group that didn't know that the others had been eager to kill Castillo.

When he crossed the threshold and glanced around, the room was empty. Curious. He could feel them, *vampiro* and humans, deeper in the club. Tori was alive, but he couldn't make the connection without letting her terror flood him. The others were cloaked, probably by Castillo, as another of his security measures. "Be careful. I think they know we're here."

Then it hit him, a wall of Tori's fear. It was so strong that he stumbled. Pain came with it, though he couldn't pinpoint its origin. He dropped his hands to his knees and bent forward, trying to block the link. He felt someone's hand on his shoulder. Someone tried to console him, but he couldn't stop the growl that rolled from his lips. "Find them. Kill them."

Someone opened the door to the back rooms. It didn't make a sound. Jonas started forward. Michael willed him to stop. When he did, Michael waved him back. "If it's a trap, I go first."

He stood straight, took a deep breath, and moved furtively into the hallway. A scream, Tori's scream, cut through the silence. His senses went into overdrive. Suddenly he could smell her in another room down the hall. Her fear was a perfume in the air, along with the tinny scent of her blood. Everything inside him screamed to calm her, but she needed to be frightened. If Castillo were feeding, he wouldn't kill her as long as she was giving him a buzz on the emotion. Besides, the fear might help her.

Michael stopped at the red painted door and motioned toward it. The teams surrounded it, guns pointed. Jonas booted it inward and went in first. Michael rushed in behind him.

His feet stopped him just beside Prince Khalil, leader of the *Council of Vampiro, Keeper of the Alleanza*. Michael offered a nod for a bow and looked for Tori.

The vampire smiled and nodded. "Evening, Michael."

Danny, one of the *vincolo* and Tori's friend, gasped behind him.

His eyes found her pinned to the ground by the prince's brother, Khamar. His heart sank. She was bleeding from what looked like four curved lines carved into her abdomen around her belly button in a sort of sadistic sun symbol.

His fists clenched.

Michael whirled around to Prince Khalil.

Castillo jumped to his feet. "What—what is this intrusion?" He turned, and his mouth fell open. "How did you..." He seemed utterly lost before he glared at Khalil. "You. You blocked their presence in my haven!"

"I've come for my *amante*, Castillo."

Khalil stayed in his place, giving little more than a glance to Castillo. "Brother, I believe your new toy belongs to Michael."

Khamar leaned back and let Tori's hands loose to hold the wound in her chest. She was pale and her hands shook, but she was alive.

"Michael, you owe her to me for Damon. If you do not leave now, you force my hand." Castillo moved closer, but not within reach of Khalil or Michael.

"We're not leaving, Castillo."

"This is your last warning." He inched closer, jabbing his finger in the air toward Michael

Michael batted it away so hard and fast that it almost made Castillo lose his footing. "No, this is *your* last warning. Give me Victoria and leave the city or I *will* kill you."

"You traitorous little...."

The Prince pushed off the wall, grabbing their attention. He walked to Tori, took her hand and pulled her gently to her feet as he spoke. "Castillo, you are bound by the *Alleanza* you like to quote so much to accept the challenge or leave."

"No, he has betrayed me many times. This is another *trucchi*."

"Shall I remind you of your deceptions? You did say that she chose you, correct?"

"Well—I." Castillo backed up, bumping into a couch as his eyes darted between Michael and their prince.

"Then it is done. You choose, Castillo. What is it to be? Give your title to the challenger and choose exile, or face the challenge."

"Challenge. I will not give my city to this *leggero*." He spit blood onto the floor at Michael's feet.

"Then prepare yourselves and clear the room. The winner gets both the city and the human."

Chapter Fifteen

TORI SAT in the chair and Khalil sat on the arm. His hand gave hers a gentle pat as Castillo's rage filled the air with an electric weight. She watched the two, but couldn't feel anything more from Michael than she already felt. He must have blocked their connection. All she could feel now was the throbbing pain from the cuts on her stomach. She glanced down. They weren't deep, but they might scar.

"We'll settle this tomorrow at—"

"No. We're not waiting." Michael pulled a gun from his waistband and handed it to Jonas. "I'm ready now, sir."

Khalil glanced at the city *padrone*. "Castillo?"

"Yes."

The room was clear of furniture now and the others stood around the perimeter. There was more than enough to create a quorum, which according to Khalil was three for a council sanctioned *Fiammifero dei Morti*, which loosely translated to Death Match. Even in Italian, the words sounded threatening.

Castillo and Michael glared at each other, moving toward the center of the room. Castillo's power erupted first and took Tori's breath in a jolt. Michael's flowed behind it, making her skin burn as it roared through her and pinged off the walls around them.

"Begin," Khalil said.

Castillo thrust a hand toward Michael and staggered backwards from the power that flowed. He cackled and moved forward for another connection, his hands clenching into fists. A wicked grin crept across his face as he threw his arm upward, slinging a fistful of power again.

Michael dodged so fast that Tori couldn't quite see it. He was suddenly standing in a different spot from where he'd been a blink before.

They both darted around the room, moving fast. All that Tori could see was an occasional blur, a group of vampires dodged them as they crashed into a cement wall so that it cracked, but they were gone again before the dust could settle onto the floor.

They stopped.

Michael was in the man's grip; Castillo's fangs planted in his shoulder.

Tori struggled against Khalil's arm. "Let me go."

He bucked, but Castillo held on and arched his back with long draws until Michael slumped in his arms.

"Michael, get up." Tori silently pleaded.

Castillo raised his head and dropped Michael to the floor. When he turned, blood dripped down his face, and his tongue worked to clean off the lips and corners of his mouth. "I've drained him, dear."

"Michael!" Tori tried to pull away, but Khalil held her tight.

Michael lay in a crumpled heap on the floor. Oozing gashes covered his chest, barely in the first stages of stitching themselves together. He didn't move. Tori closed her eyes. She couldn't feel him. With a deep breath, she exhaled and pushed her mind toward him, trying to find that connection.

"Give her to me," Castillo said. His footfalls were coming closer.

"Please, Michael." Tori whispered the words as she pushed harder to reach him.

Then she felt it, a faint buzz at first. She wound up all the strength she could and pushed it toward him. The connection grew stronger, but she felt herself fall against Khalil.

There was movement and a gasp.

She opened her eyes in time to see Michael leap forward. He tackled Castillo's back, sinking his teeth into the man's neck. Castillo screamed and thrashed, then sunk his nails into Michael's sides. Power exploded from them. The lights overhead flickered and went out in a shower of glass. Tori felt herself swaying on her feet. A woman screamed in the darkness, but she closed her eyes and tried to will Michael more strength.

* * * *

Michael's back smashed into the wall. He groaned, but continued to drink from Castillo, taking in that soured metallic taste of his blood. The life was draining out of him in slow segments that made Michael want to pull away and heave the putrid taste of the man from his body. Still, he jumped and bucked, slowing with each draining pull until finally, his body stopped moving. Another drink and he went limp. Michael sucked harder. There was no second chance. If he didn't drink it all and take in Castillo's power quickly, then his place as the new *padrone* would be open to challenge by every *neonato* in the country.

He drank another long draw and felt the life begin to loosen. He pulled, and it flowed to him with the blood, but it wasn't just the power. It was Castillo, the soul. Horror shook him and almost took the body from his grip, but Michael managed to drink again.

Flashes of people, places, and death came at him so fast that he couldn't see them all. They weighed heavy in his chest like a bad meal, but he forced himself to continue until it was done. When there was nothing left in the corpse, Michael dropped it to the floor and wiped his mouth with the back of his hand.

He opened his eyes to see that his crew had lit the flashlights. He motioned to the body. "Get rid of it."

The Serpentine group grabbed the body and left the room. There was no mention of their intent. Michael didn't think he wanted to know their plans. There was probably some ritual involving consumption to try to take his power into them, but there was nothing left. They'd find it out soon enough.

Khalil still held Tori by the arm as he glared at Castillo's entourage. "Any of you who stay will obey Michael's rule and the judgment of the Council. He is not like Castillo. If you break the *Alleanza*, you will die. Go now and make your decision by the next sunset. Tomorrow night I will expect you to leave or swear your allegiance to the *padrone*." Khalil cleared his throat. "This is a legal exchange. Michael has been a fair and honest brother, and I will take his word as truth. Anyone who fails to follow his new regime will be subject to the *Caccia di Anima*."

Castillo's group bowed quickly, then scattered. There were no footsteps to tell them where they'd gone, but he could feel them fleeing the club, just as he could feel his connection to Tori. Castillo must have bound them all to him, since they weren't his own progeny.

Khalil smiled. "You realize that they'll never be loyal to you."

"Yes."

"Always the practical one." Khalil laughed. "This will be an interesting exchange."

"I'm glad she came along to move you to action." He let go of Tori's arm. "The council has discussed the possibility of your *coup d'état* many times. Glad to see it is finally here."

Michael flinched, then smiled as Tori crashed into his chest. "Thank you."

"We will expect to see you at the next meeting. It is in your best interest to pay a visit to the Council. Perhaps to secure your power with Castillo's allies."

"When is it?"

"January. In Venice."

"I'll be there."

Khamar left the room, never quite looking Michael in the eye.

"If you will excuse us, Khamar and I have other business to attend to. Expect a formal apology from him soon. I cannot curb my brother's tastes, but I will not allow this injustice to stand with your *amante*." Just as Khalil neared the door, he turned once more. "Oh, bring her with you. She is a nice addition. A strong one."

Michael gave them a small bow of the head. "Consider it done." He smiled down at Tori. She was covered in blood and her eyes were puffy from crying, but she was beautiful. He hadn't had time to notice before, but the *vincolare* had changed her, taken the tension out of her eyes and replaced it with a softness that he'd never seen before. "Ready to go home?"

She nodded.

"Go wait in the car. We need to clean up here first."

"Let me help."

"I don't think you want to see this." Michael held her face in his hands. "Castillo kept a lot of *blood mystresses*. Some of them can't be saved."

When she didn't argue, he knew she understood.

He kissed her softly on the cheek. "I won't be long."

"Promise?"

"Promise." He smiled and backed away. He'd been waiting to see that look on her face for years and it made his heart warm. No one had looked at him like that in so long that he'd begun to think it was a blessing that came only once in a life. Now, seeing it on Tori's face and feeling how her will had softened to him, he knew that no one deserved to feel it more than once.

* * * *

Tori watched Michael turn and leave the room with the others tight on his heels. Jonas stayed with her, but they both stood silent. He must have seen the difference in Michael, too. He walked with even more confidence and seemed to radiate power. But, there was something else—something darker that seemed like an invisible warning beacon. In killing Castillo, he'd become much more dangerous.

"He took his power," Jonas said in a quiet voice. "Do you feel it?"

"Yeah."

"He'll need to feed more often now, at least to begin with." He glanced at her. "Are you okay with that?"

"I'm his *amante*, Jonas. I'll do whatever he needs." She moved toward the hallway and he followed.

"Glad to see that you finally admit it."

She smirked. "Don't rub it in."

They moved into the private bar. It was deserted, except for the light from Jonas' flashlight. The place had always seemed scary, but now in the dark silence, it seemed downright macabre. She half expected someone to jump out of the shadows like in the horror flicks.

Once they moved into the larger bar, he caught up to walk beside her. "So, you're going to be our *padrone's amante*. Any chance you're turning?"

"Hell no."

She glanced down at the dry blood that covered her abdomen.

"It should heal fast, especially now."

She nodded. "I think you're right."

They made their way outside in silence. With each step, they were farther from Michael. Just her and Jonas. She wouldn't have dared to be outside alone at night with him before now. He seemed nice enough, but no one could convince her that Jonas wasn't one hundred percent interested in anything other than sex and her blood. He'd never hidden it, though she expected that the bond with Michael would put an end to the openness.

"You sit in the car. I'll stay out here and make sure none of Castillo's guys come around." He slipped his cell phone from his pocket and handed it to her. "Don't you think you need to call the Chief?"

She nodded. "Yeah, I'll do that." She gave him a quick pat on the shoulder. "Thanks."

Tori walked to the black SUV. She opened the back passenger door first, to make sure no one was hiding in there, then opened the front passenger seat and slid inside. The vehicle shut out the sounds and left her with the roaring of her connection with Michael and his new power. It was distracting, but in time, it would become background noise. Hopefully the emotional connection they shared, how she'd always imagined it would feel to find her soul mate, would never become background noise. The thought was frightening but more so was the idea that Michael might someday realize he needed more than a human.

She shook her head. She wasn't going to do this. Not now. They were bonded, and that had to be enough. She wouldn't ruin what could be a little bit of peace in her life by worrying about the future. Not this time. It always ended too quickly, so she would enjoy it now. Robert's death had taught her that.

Chapter Sixteen

SHE FELT Michael coming closer, glanced to the front door of the club, and saw him emerge. He smiled at her immediately, as though he could see her through the dark tinted windows.

He and Jonas were talking as they moved closer. When they reached the vehicle, Jonas slid into the back seat and Michael came around to the driver's side. The door opened and he slid in, bringing with him that wonderful, familiar scent.

Tori smiled. She didn't need the connection to know what he had in mind.

The rest of the ride was in virtual silence. Except for the occasional small talk that Jonas attempted to break the silence, the short trip from *The Scene* to *The Fallen* was comprised of glances, smiles, and soft strokes of Michael's hand over hers. They didn't need words now. She felt his thoughts, the mix of adoration and lust that swirled like a torrent just under the thin fabric of their silence. They'd always had something, but the bond made it so much more. There was no inhibition now, no reason not to trust, when every emotion was there for the other to feel on a level that words could never express.

"Wait here," Michael said aloud as he pushed the shifter into park at the club's lot. He bounded out before Jonas could step out and hurried around to her side. He opened her door and offered his hand.

She took it and stepped out onto the pavement. As he handed the keys to Jonas, she noticed something different in his face. When he turned toward her again, he smiled. That was it. He wasn't masking. She'd never seen him this relaxed. Before there had always been the mask of power to keep her from seeing his real face, the one with expressions that matched the emotions. Now, it was there, and it made him seem more human.

They slipped into the private bar through the side entrance, where a full crowd gathered. Someone began to clap and then others joined in. There were cheers, whistles, and someone calling Michael's name. News spread fast, even in the vampire world.

"Michael!" One of the bimbos bounced over toward them.

Tori jumped in front of him so fast that she felt dizzy. She heard Jonas gasp as she snarled at the woman.

The girl blinked and tried to go around her. "He knows me."

She moved into the woman's face and felt Michael's hands on her shoulders softly urging her backward. They were definitely going to cause a scene, but Tori couldn't stop herself. She was furious, filled with a rage she'd never known before. Jealousy didn't begin to describe it. It was more like how she imagined a mother might feel when her child is threatened. All her nerves felt alive and she couldn't stop if she wanted to. "If you want to keep that bleached blonde hair in your head, you'll walk away. Now!"

The woman's mouth fell open, and she just watched as Michael dragged her carefully toward the private hallway. He whispered Italian words in her ear as she watched the woman—no, the competitor—who'd had her hands all over his body. Tori wasn't stupid. The woman had probably shared his bed and her blood with him.

Tori let out a long shriek and tried to pull away from him.

Nothing but space separated them. If she could get her hands on the girl, there wouldn't be a reminder for Michael. No bimbos in his club.

Then something cracked inside her head. She didn't understand it all, but knew that he was trying to push back the blood-red rage. When they were on the other side of the door, the jealousy subsided and she let out a long breath. The inferno in her head was replaced with the cool calm of his power.

"Better?" He pushed the door open and motioned her inside.

She nodded. "Did I make a total fool of myself?"

He laughed and the sound echoed off the walls as he shut the door. "I don't think anyone noticed but her. We'll just have to work on it."

"A side effect?"

"Another part of our bond." He took her hand again and led her down the secret staircase toward his private chamber. "All of your emotions will be stronger, but our protective instincts toward each other will be magnified. I feel the same way about you."

She followed him down the stairs closely. "When?"

"Like when Jonas was walking behind you in the hallway."

She let out a small laugh.

He shrugged and opened the door to the main room. He shut it after they walked through, and followed her to his room with his hand on the small of her back. He grabbed that door, opened it, and then pulled it shut behind them. "Is everything settled with the police?"

"I think the Chief will let it go. I just told him that I fatally wounded Damon and that they took off." It was a lie, but the Chief would never believe the truth. Besides, they needed a way to make Damon's death legal to end the hunt for the serial killer. "They'll search for him for a while. I hope your guys hid him well."

Michael laughed. "He'll never be found." He gave her a soft, short kiss, and then turned to walk away. "I love you, *inamorato.*"

Tori moved to the bathroom door. Her legs ached and her stomach burned.

Michael smiled at her from the end of the counter, where he folded clothes and put them on the granite.

"I'm glad it's over." She stripped the shirt over her head carefully. They both looked battle-scarred and worn from the fight, covered in dry blood and cuts, but he made it look good.

He folded his arms across his chest and leaned his back against the wall, eyeing her. "Me too, because now you're mine."

She took the pants off carefully and watched him watching her. It would have been nice to do a sexy kind of strip, but Tori's muscles were sore and it was all she could manage not to fall flat on her face as she took off the clothes and stepped into the shower. "You getting in?"

"Go ahead."

She let the water wash down her back first, then soak her hair. "Thanks for starting the shower."

"No problem." Michael's voice sounded like he was smiling.

She covered the cuts on her stomach and turned toward the water to let it wash her chest, too. When she turned back, Michael was smiling down at her. She jumped back and gasped, then immediately swiped her hand at his chest in a playful slap. "Don't do that."

"I just saved your life. You shouldn't hit me."

She wrapped her arms around his waist and settled her face against his chest. "Thank you for that."

"I wouldn't have dreamed of leaving you there."

"Speaking of Castillo, did Khalil really help us tonight?"

"I don't know."

"You should've asked."

He laughed. "You don't ask the *Padrone* of all free vampires if he helped when it's forbidden by the council, you just assume he did and never bring it up again."

"I thought he was top dog. What does the council matter?"

"He is to the council what the President is to Congress. They can and will punish him for disobeying, though my kin take their punishments in blood and flesh."

She kissed the scar on his chest, the one from the silver. It was a scar he'd taken for her. She smiled up at him, and then leaned up to meet his lips.

When they met, he gave her a slow, probing kiss. His hands moved to her hair and held her face as he bit slowly, gently on her bottom lip. When she sighed, he smiled. "You realize you still owe me."

She thought for a moment. "The *affascinare*? I thought we'd done that."

"Anything you've felt is because of our bond and your own emotions." He held her face as he stared into her eyes. "So, I'm taking that payment now."

Michael's power rolled down her body, pulling chills as it went. Her breath caught, and she felt as though they were lifting off the floor. Her head was light, drunk in his power. When it reached her midsection, her body tensed. She could feel the warmth growing between her legs. Inside, everything but the need faded away, like thirst on a hot summer's day, and it consumed her. Each touch of his fingers set her skin alight. She could almost feel the glow of it.

Her knees buckled but he caught her and pulled her tight against him. He felt so good, so strong, and she could feel his excitement pressing against her belly. There was no holding back now. Her hands pushed up his chest. She lingered there on the expanse of muscle that enveloped her, then moved to his neck. Her fingers gripped the back of his head and pulled him down to a deep kiss that made his sharp teeth nick her bottom lip.

He pulled back. His eyes darkened with need and his lips parted slightly, coated with a thin film of her blood. He was magnificent.

She leaned forward to take his lips again and felt his lust flare suddenly into a blinding force that made her arch her body against his chest.

He moved, forcing her to chase his lips as he lifted her.

She wrapped her legs around him and buried her face in his neck, kissing and sucking at the skin. The shower cut off behind her, and she felt him walk them into the bathroom. It was chilly, but the heat off his body made her warm enough to ignore it while she nibbled hard enough to make him groan.

"The *trucchi*'s supposed to work only on you." He walked slowly into the bedroom, running his hands up and down her thighs. "I think it's taking both of us."

She smelled vanilla and glanced up long enough to note the candles that lit the room in preparation for her. Any other time, she'd be mad at his assumption, but tonight she was glad of it. She didn't want to pretend anymore.

Her lips went back to his neck. This time she caught something between her lips. His pulse beat against her tongue and she could almost taste his blood. She knew the feeling was his, but it still made her want to bite down.

Michael groaned, almost stopping in mid-step.

On his knees, he carefully climbed them onto the bed while she kissed her way to his mouth. He pulled her back again to look at her. "Do you want me to stop? Our bond made this stronger than I intended."

"No." She panted, trying to kiss him again.

He used her hair to pull her back enough to look at him. "Victoria."

"Don't stop. Please." She looked into his eyes, falling again into that dark abyss, and willed her feelings toward him. The need for his touch, to feel him take her was like an unbearable flame coursing through her veins. If he only knew, he wouldn't ask.

"You're not yourself."

"I am, now more than ever. I need you, *amante*."

He let out a low growl at the sound of her using their word. He took her mouth in a forceful kiss. His arms pulled her legs around his waist, as her lips pressed hard against his mouth. He groaned and kissed his way toward her neck with her firmly on his lap. His erection twitched between them.

Tori ground her body against him, rubbing him in slow moves.

"I'm not going to last long," he whispered, then took a bit of her neck between his teeth.

"Me either," she said, panting. "I want it. All of it."

His body twitched as he scratched his fangs down the side of her neck.

She shivered, and then used her arms on his shoulders to pull herself up. When she slid back down, his flesh impaled her slowly.

They moaned together.

"Yes, Michael."

He wrapped his hand in her hair and pulled her neck to one side as Tori ground her hips down on him. Her body tightened and she could feel the orgasm building. Her heart felt like it would burst from pure adulation, but her body smoldered with a hunger for both his blood and his skin.

Another rush of his power flowed over her. Her back arched and she threw her head back.

His mouth clamped down on her. When his teeth penetrated her flesh, the crest broke, sending her into an otherworldly place where her body was no longer hers. She could feel him drinking from her and each draw brought another, stronger crest until she screamed and felt herself clawing at his back, but she couldn't stop. It was the closest she'd ever come to an out-of-body experience, just like all those psychic idiots always talked about on television.

When she came back into herself, Michael was shuddering against her. His teeth pulled from her and his tongue slipped over the wound quickly, giving her smaller aftershocks. She heard herself laughing as he laid her back on the bed.

"Are you okay?" He said, smiling down at her.

She nodded, panting with a frivolous grin on her face.

He kissed her softly and lay down beside her. He propped himself up on one elbow and looked down at her, as his free hand stroked a slow path from her hip to her stomach and then over her breast.

"I love you." The funny thing was—she meant it.

Michael blinked back down at her, then smiled. He kissed her on the forehead, then leaned back and looked at the scar on her neck. His finger stroked it lightly. "You've had my heart since before Robert was turned, *inamorato*."

She gave him a questioning look. "What does that mean?"

"*Inamorato*?"

"Yes." Her breathing was beginning to slow again.

"Sweetheart."

"And when is it that I was supposed to have stolen your heart?"

He smiled again and gave off nervous energy that made her stomach flutter. "I was in charge of researching Robert for Castillo and met you once."

"When?"

"You came to the club to check on him and I bought you a drink at the bar."

She still couldn't stop smiling at him. "That was you?"

He nodded. "I've been looking out for you ever since. Didn't you wonder how we got to you so quickly when you were attacked?"

"I haven't had time to think about it since I found out about our *vincolo*."

"I was there. Outside. Waiting to make sure he didn't turn on you."

There were flashes, images of her and Robert, and of him attacking her. They were Michael's memories -- memories of bursting in and slamming Robert into the wall. Then there was stillness. He was feeding her, coaxing her back with gentle words.

Warmth expanded in her chest and filled her. She leaned forward and kissed him again. "My guardian angel. Just like your name."

He kissed her, then snuggled in, wrapping her in his arms.

"Do you think it will work? For us, I mean?"

"Some of Castillo's people will challenge it, but we're stronger." He kissed her cheek. "As long as you're with me, it will be fine."

"I'm not going anywhere." She said the words, but it wasn't until they finished echoing in the room that she knew that it was true. Even as her eyes closed and sleep began to numb her mind, she repeated the words in her head. She wasn't going anywhere.

* * * *

Tori pulled her arms close to her chest and watched as Gregory, Blane, Jonas, and Jack carried Christine's casket from the long black hearse with their heads hung low. She

realized how different they all looked in dark suits, trudg-
ing through the pale glow of the full moon where it filtered
through the willows and oaks around them. The shadows on
their faces made them look even more predatory and their
eyes took on a threatening sparkle.

Not everyone looked so menacing. Michael looked even
more human when she looked up at him. It helped that he
smiled down at her, but hid the long canines.

She'd missed him. The two days and nights following
Castillo's death were a blur of clean ups, picking up neces-
sities and Blade from her apartment, and meetings with the
Chief. Since she'd done a "superior" job, he'd granted her
request for a week off, but she and Michael hadn't spent
much time together, which was why she'd eagerly come to
the funeral they'd arranged for Christine. Even the telepathic
link they shared had to be blocked until they had a chance to
work on it. The random flashes of thought and memory had
been overwhelming, mostly for her.

The groundskeeper, funeral home owner, and other vampires followed as the guys moved forward and placed the
coffin onto the lowering straps. When it was secure, Gregory
moved to the head of the oak casket that lay perched over
the grave, while the groundskeeper placed a long spray of
crimson roses on top.

Michael put his arms around her and the warmth from his
chest helped steady her. It wasn't cold, but being in a grave-
yard in the middle of the night with a *cosca* of vampires had
a way of chilling a person. They were her friends and family
now, but they were still a dangerous group. They were all
killers and, under the right circumstances, would drain her
dry, but she was learning to understand them. They loved
their leader, almost as much as she did.

As Gregory laid a rose on top of the wood beside the large
spread of crimson flowers, he said, "Christine wouldn't have
wanted us to do a long service. She would have thought it

was unnecessary and pompous. So, I thought it would be best if I read one of her favorite poems in her honor: *A Death Wish*, by Samuel Taylor Coleridge." Gregory cleared his voice. "Come, come, thou bleak December wind, and blow the dry leaves from the tree! Flash, like a love-thought, thro' me, Death and take a life, that wearies me."

"Congratulations, *fratello*," Jonas muttered, but was soon joined in by the other vampires.

Tori barely heard the words, but it wrenched her heart just the same. She couldn't agree with the others, even though Christine had always treated her like a second-class citizen. She was a life, one that meant something to those who had known her. Her death, especially at Damon's hands, was tragic. Somehow, the vampires seemed to find it a cause for celebration. Perhaps it was their way, to honor their dead and their journey into whatever awaited them all in the next realm. After living for hundreds of years in this life, maybe true death wasn't a bad thing.

"We'll finish up at the bar. The entire cosca will be in mourning tonight, so no feeding." Michael pulled his arms away from Tori, then took her hand and led her toward the limo parked beneath a towering oak. "I expect everyone to be there."

Tori walked with him, careful not to step on the graves that she could see. "That's it?"

"That's all that's necessary. Anything we had to say should have been said before she died."

"No prayers?"

"Christine wasn't a religious person. She wouldn't have wanted it."

"Weird."

Michael opened the door to the limo for her. "Only if you're human. When you've been alive for more than a century, it's not so strange."

Tori climbed into the automobile and waited for him to get in. They rode, along with Jonas and Jude, back to the apartment. They listened as Jonas recited the offers Michael had coming in from the other families, but didn't speak. Instead, they held hands and stole glances while they tried to look like they were interested in what he was saying.

At the club, Michael went to his office, but Tori moved to his room to change. When she opened the door, the room was filled with the scent of the roses that decorated the room and vanilla candles that rested on most of the surfaces. She smiled.

She opened the top drawer of the highboy chest, her drawer, and pulled out a pair of worn jeans and a white British flag T-shirt. They weren't exactly appropriate, but they were comfortable and her favorites.

It didn't take long to change, so she moved back up to the private bar. The sound of guitars being tuned and mic checks filled the room from the open door dividing the VIP area from the rest of the club. Gregory and Blane sat at a table in front of them in bouncer uniforms, shooting a paper football back and forth at each other. The two had become her assigned bodyguards. Of course, she'd argued with Michael about it, but there was no swaying him. So, the guys followed her everywhere when he wasn't around.

Jack smiled from behind the bar, where he stood along with the waitresses and Jude, who kept watching her with a weird grin on her face. "What can I get ya, Tori?"

"Jack and Coke."

He nodded and started working on the order as she hopped up to sit on the bar with her legs dangling over the side, her knees spread. "You know, you surprise me."

"Why?"

"I thought you'd run after he took out Castillo. Seen too much of the bad stuff. But you're alright, human. You just might make it."

"Thanks." She took the drink as he slid it onto the counter. "I think."

As others filtered into the room, she took a long drink. She licked the liquid from her lips just as Michael walked in. He moved to stand in front of her, leaning between her knees with his back to her. She didn't see it, but she knew he was smiling and thinking dirty thoughts. She felt it and grinned, too.

"We need to start the meeting. We open at midnight," he said.

Alana, a petite dark-haired woman in a business suit, sat farther down the bar and spoke quietly with Danny, her human boyfriend. The others were scattered around the room in small clusters, but she didn't know most of them. Among those nine, there were two men in suits, a woman in scrubs, a couple covered in tattoos, a man in a state trooper uniform, and the last three were young women who looked like twenty-year-old blonde sorority types. They resembled each other so much, they may have even been sisters. Either Michael had turned a lot of people in his time, or he'd taken in a lot of strays. Her bet was on the latter.

Jonas stood to Michael's right, leaned back on his elbow, one of which was against Tori's thigh. He wore a black T-shirt that hugged his muscles and accentuated his broad shoulders. On the back was a set of white crosshairs with the words: *Go ahead, but you'd better fucking kill me.*

He twisted his head to her and gave her a sly smile and wink.

Tori laughed and shook her head. Somehow, he always seemed to know when she was looking at him and confronted it with a wink or a blown kiss. But she couldn't stop. Taking Michael's vein and creating the bond made her feel his affection for the man that he called his brother. Only, with Jonas' innate sensuality and his power over females, she didn't exactly want to be his sister when he strutted past her in the tight leathers he wore to perform. They'd definitely have to work on that. Soon.

Michael looked at Jonas, then cut his eyes back to her. There was nothing humorous in the look.

Shit. She gave him a squeeze with her thighs and he rubbed his hand down her leg. She'd have to avoid Jonas until she learned to navigate her new emotions.

Michael cleared his throat and everyone quieted. "Thank you for coming. I wanted to talk with you before I made a few decisions that will affect all of us." He stood a little straighter. "You all know that I've inherited all of Castillo's property. The club is the first order of business. *The Scene*, I believe, will be best run under Jonas' hand, if he will accept it."

The two men shared a look that Tori couldn't read, then Jonas smiled. "Sure. I'll do it."

Tori gave him a pat on the shoulder and smiled when he glanced at her. It was the perfect match.

"Now, since I'm going to be *padrone*, I need a *Garante*," Michael said. "After careful consideration, I would like to also offer this position to Jonas."

"You mean you just want to tape a bull's-eye on my ass."

Michael and the others laughed. "Look at it this way, you'll be getting paid to fight and all the women will think you're tough."

Jonas smiled. "Good enough."

"I also need a liaison to work with the other families. I need this person to have a great deal of patience and tact. Since she puts up with you, Danny, I thought Alana would be perfect."

"Hey." Danny feigned offense. "I—uh—never mind. You have a point."

Alana laughed, then smiled and gave Michael a graceful nod. "I would be honored."

"Good. Sienna, Hope, and Beth, you're in charge of events planning. We'll have to host Khalil at some point as well as the usual celebrations."

The sorority girls were giddy at the prospect. The middle one said, "Thank you, Michael."

"I'm going to need advisors for finances. That's where I need you two, Stewart and Perry." The suits nodded. "Jack Knife and Rose, you're going to handle information gathering, with Mag." The tattooed people nodded, as did the cop. "And Marie, I need you to do what you always do. Patch us all up." The doctor nodded, too. "Everyone else knows what their job is. The last thing I wanted to say is that I've also decided to move into Castillo's mansion."

Michael stiffened as the others groaned. "I understand your disappointment, but the compound has excellent security and—well—I need the room, because I was hoping that Victoria would move in with me."

Tori didn't try to fight the smile on her face. Her heart pounded. She was going to move in with Michael. Not only that, but into a mansion. The guys in the department would never believe it.

No, they wouldn't.

In fact, it would be so unlikely that they'd probably put I.A. on her for money laundering or some stupid shit like that. She'd have to keep it quiet. Real quiet. Hell, it might not even work, but she wasn't going to pass up moving in with him because of it. Even if it meant quitting her job. If she had to, she'd just open her own investigation firm.

"That's not fair." One of the waitresses moved up behind Tori. "This is home."

Michael glanced at her, but didn't have a chance to answer because Blane chimed in. "This has been *our* home for decades. You're our *cosca* and without you here, it won't be the same."

"Yeah," Jonas said.

Tori could feel Michael thinking. He was trying to be diplomatic, but she knew he wouldn't budge on this. "Wait... how much room is there at the compound?"

Michael and Jonas looked at her, but the latter answered. "A lot. That place is a friggin' fortress."

"Enough for everyone to move in?"

"If they want," Michael said, squeezing her knee softly. He turned to the group again. "You're all welcome to move with me. I just thought you'd be ready to get rid of me after all these years."

"Well, now that you mention it...."

Michael punched Jonas in the shoulder, which started a mock fight.

She watched them play like real brothers, and it made her heart swell with a feeling that she could only describe as love. They were family now, her new family. She could never go back to that old life, the one where she slept alone every night, afraid of the shadows, and took pills to sleep. She was Michael's *amante*, and this was where she belonged. She wasn't just a human anymore, and hadn't been in a very long time.

He turned between Tori's legs to face her. "Well?"

"What?"

"Will you move in with me, *inamorato*?" His hand wrapped around hers, and his face held all the sincerity of a man proposing something much greater.

It was now or never. "Yes."

He pulled her to him and into a soft, slow kiss. A brush of warm lips that made her insides melt into quivering goo. There were few perfect moments in life, and this was one of them, so she wouldn't push. She'd let him control the kiss, and let it be what it was because life was starting to be much more fun when she just let it happen.

Behind Michael, someone wolf-whistled. The others laughed and jeered, and Danny yelled, "Get a room!"

THE END

Also Available from Red Silk Editions

Blood & Sex: Michael
by Angela Cameron

This is a spine-chilling and erotic tale of a Mafia vampire and the detective who is determined to bring to justice a serial killer. Detective Victoria Tyler allows Mafia vampire Michael to "take her neck" and lead her on a journey through a world of bondage, domination, and blood to stop the killer. But can she resist the dark lusts he sparks?

Volume 1 in the Blood & Sex series

Paperback: $12.95

978-1-59003-203-9

Available in August 2010

Blood & Sex: Jonas
by Angela Cameron

Jonas, the strangely appealing owner of the new vampire-themed bondage club could be the perfect distraction for workaholic Dr. Elena Jensen. But their worlds couldn't be farther apart....

Volume 2 of the Blood & Sex series

Paperback: $12.95

978-1-59003-202-2

Available in October 2010

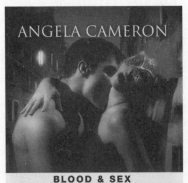

Blood & Sex: Blane
by Angela Cameron

Will Blane be able to break through the guarded reserve of Christiana, the beautiful woman the vampire leader has sent to educate the newest vampires? Or will her sense of duty be stronger than the passion that threatens to sweep her away?

Volume 3 of the Blood & Sex series

Paperback: $12.95

978-1-59003-206-0

Available in December 2010

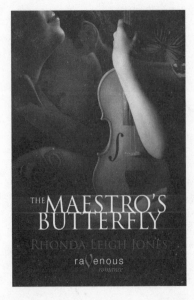

The Maestro's Butterfly
by Rhonda Leigh Jones

Miranda O'Connell has just made a dangerous bet with her mysterious, sexy music teacher that will change her life forever. Will she fall in love with the kinky vampire Maestro and submit to life as a feeder slave? Or will she escape the confines of his estate for the dashing, dangerous charms of his brother?

Paperback: $12.95

978-1-59003-207-7

Available in November 2010

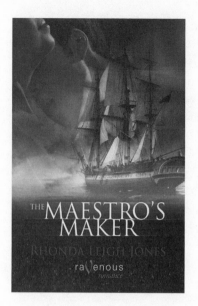

The Maestro's Maker
by Rhonda Leigh Jones

Trapped between two vampires: Chloe discovers the darkness that binds the beautiful and arrogant French noble Claudio du Fresne and his oldest friend Francois Villaforte. With danger, intrigue, and kinky sex, *The Maestro's Maker* takes vampire erotica to passionate new levels!

Paperback: $12.95

978-1-59003-210-7

Available in December 2010

The Maestro's Apprentice
by Rhonda Leigh Jones

For the first time in her life, Autumn is free. She has escaped Claudio du Fresne, the vampire for whom she had been a feeder-slave for years. Now she wants to play, and for her, playing means wild, crazy sex with strangers.

Paperback: $12.95

978-1-59003-209-1

Available in January 2011

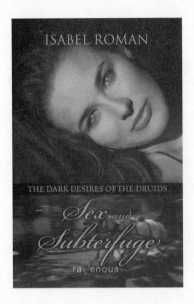

The Dark Desires of the Druids:
Sex & Subterfuge
by Isabel Roman

"Do you like jealous heroes and love triangles? How about sizzling sexual encounters atop dining room furniture? If you answered yes to either question, you're going to love this novella."
—Susan S., loveromance.passion.com

Paperback: $12.95

978-1-59003-200-8

Available in August 2010

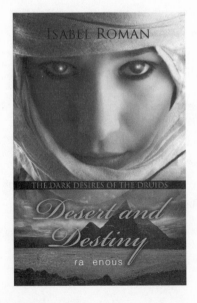

The Dark Desires of the Druids:
Desert and Destiny
by Isabel Roman

The first time they met, Arbelle Bahari tried to kill him. The second time, they made love on a desk in the British Museum.

"The action is fast and exciting, the mystery is engaging, and the romance is searingly hot." —*Whipped Cream Reviews* (5 Cherries)

Paperback: $12.95

978-1-59003-201-5

Available in October 2010

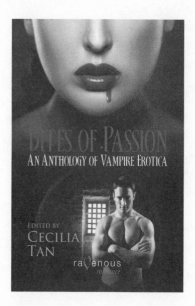

Bites of Passion
edited by Cecilia Tan

What does it mean to love a vampire? Does it mean nights of pleasure tempered with sweet pain? Eight top authors explore the themes of immortal love, the lust for blood, and the eternal struggle between light and dark.

Paperback: $12.95

978-1-59003-205-3

Available in September 2010

Magic University: The Siren and the Sword
by Cecilia Tan

Harvard freshman Kyle Wadsorth is eager to start a new life. Surprises abound when he discovers a secret magical university hidden inside Harvard and he meets Jess Torralva, who tutors him in the ways of magic, sex, and love.

Paperback: $12.95

978-1-59003-208-4

Available in November 2010

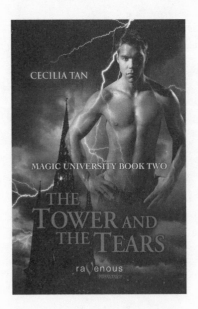

Magic University: The Tower and the Tears by Cecilia Tan

This second volume in the Magic University series brings together myth, magic, and eroticism for adult readers of fantasy who want a bedtime tale of their own.

"Simply one of the most important writers, editors, and innovators in contemporary American erotic literature." — Susie Bright

Paperback: $12.95

978-1-59003-211-4

Available in January 2011

Mind Games by Cecilia Tan

Who hasn't fantasized about using psychic abilities to satisfy your every sexual desire? *Mind Games* provides readers the opportunity to live out that dream....

"Scorching hot with a touch of suspense. Cecilia Tan brings together love, suspense, and scorching sex in a story well worth reading." — *ParaNormal Romance Review*

Paperback: $12.95

978-1-59003-204-6

Available in September 2010